RADIANCE

RADIANCE

a NOVEL

LOUIS B. JONES

COUNTERPOINT
BERKELEY

Library of Congress Cataloging-in-Publication Data

Jones, Louis B.
  Radiance : a novel / Louis B. Jones.
    p. cm.
  ISBN 978-1-58243-736-1
  1. College teachers--Fiction. 2. Physicists--Fiction. 3. Lyme disease--Patients--Fiction. 4. Fathers and daughters--Fiction. 5. California--Fiction. 6. Psychological fiction. 7. Domestic fiction. I. Title.
  PS3560.O516R33 2011
  813'.54--dc22
                        2011002822

Cover design by Silverander Communications
Interior design by Megan Jones Design
Printed in the United States of America

COUNTERPOINT
1919 Fifth Street
Berkeley, CA 94710

www.counterpointpress.com

Distributed by Publishers Group West

10 9 8 7 6 5 4 3 2 1

★ DEATH—NOT SOME SPOOKY or religious or abstract idea of it but just the practical everyday ingredient in nature—is everywhere close, everywhere a comfortable, cool medium to thrive in, right against the skin as it is. At an age that struck him as premature (forty-two), a certain nondescript, unremarkable ordinary person (named Mark Perdue, an academic physicist who happened to be visiting Los Angeles) was having this surprisingly serene, commonplace realization, that when death does come—if not right this minute, then someday—it will turn out to feel rather like the solution at the end of an old math problem; it won't necessarily be a wrenching experience, or even an unhappy experience. At the point of finally giving up oneself (one's most cherished so-called self), it will come perfectly *naturally* for a man to—like water droplets appearing out of nothing—resolve again into the elements.

He opened his palm in air combing atmosphere. Death abides always there in constant contact, right at one's fingertips, in the form of the Periodic Table of Elements' basic, cool powders and metals and crystals and colorless odors, while the sensation of *"life"* is merely the rarest, briefest tingle, throughout all the galaxies' endless tonnage. Great, cold womb. Mineral of all germination. Death is oxygen, it's not only cobalt and zinc, it's also nitrogen and carbon. Death is the

1

clear sky of an ordinary day, nitrogen blue at wavelength 475 nm in the visible spectrum. Brilliant death, structural death, life is death: *"consciousness"* can't even string together the pebbles and dusts of this universal ore, not really. At every motion of "consciousness," mortality intervenes, eternity intervenes, in every moment, too quick for the eye, in a billion consecutive brainflashes, like a deck-of-cards shuffle, so time and consciousness may *seem* to travel continuously and fluidly. As if there were no blackouts flickering between. As if there were no new personalities incarnated between. As if there were always a consistent "self," or "soul," freestanding as a Doric column.

These were the panoply of commonplace old facts that whirled in the face of "Mark Perdue," physics professor visiting from out of town, while he pressed his elbows in farewell upon the wooden armrests of his auditorium seat in L.A. At this moment, his overriding *practical* interest was in distinguishing between a heart attack's genuine symptoms and its imaginary symptoms—because there might be an unavoidable short bit of pain or embarrassment on the way out. It is common knowledge that a sharp little discomfort precisely in the area of the heart isn't necessarily a coronary. Real coronaries involve more widespread signs. All he had was the chest pressure. He had no arm pain, no shortness of breath, no cold sweat. And forty-two is too young, too young for anything but the imaginary sort of heart attack, *envisioned* in such detail that the idea can get a grip. And ever since his one big bout with Lyme disease, he has been borne up, regularly, by a bouncy fizz of bizarre nervous twinges and zaps and clanging sensations that, if alarming, or sometimes truly stupefying, amount to nothing.

Nevertheless, the pure idea of a heart attack does, suddenly, lift a man upon a pinnacle. Because death, one thing to be said for it is that it's a sure thing. It's foolproof. And given the circumstances, here in L.A., an efficient little heart attack (a basically thrifty little heart attack if it succeeds) could make sense: Los Angeles is a fatiguing, jarring place, during a hectic weekend for a visitor to be deprived of his accustomed daily routine, far from his usual comforts, far from the assigned parking place in the faculty lot in Berkeley, far from his regular pastry while he hides out at Cafe Med off-campus and afterward his own office's tarnished sticky doorknob, far from the pervasive campus air of eucalyptus, the smell of blackboard-eraser talcum in the corridors: all are familiar daily medicines *preventing* heart attacks, all habits to keep a man on paths in life *veering* from any heart attacks.

Instead, now, here was Mark Perdue physically, bodily, in faraway Los Angeles sitting in row 7, seat GG, in a very loud concert hall—his daughter had at last mounted the stage, and she'd cued the band with a wink and gone straight into her song—which ought to have been a moment of accomplishment, and lapse, and relief. But that was when he started to think the fixed feeling in his ribs could be the onset, the sensation of an anvil, taking shape inside his chest. And he thought back to the beginning of the weekend, boarding the plane, when he'd felt this exact same discomfort in the heart and might have foreseen this. In a way, he did foresee it.

He and his daughter, among the SFO–LAX commuters Friday morning, had been shuffling along dragging their carry-ons inside the drafty, dirty telescope that connects terminal and airplane, when he'd felt in his chest the first sigh, the first dilation, the immortal sadness, and he did foresee this whole thing (if only in the misty way one foresees all futures, all possibilities, all consequences and ramifications, omnisciently, the consciousness always editing, among the collapsing wave functions), but he set it aside. He set it aside just as one sets aside an infinite number of possible futures. There were plenty of people lined up behind him to board the plane. And it's true: he's too young for a heart attack. And who wants to make a fuss and disturb the queue, once you've slipped through with your boarding pass and your carry-on so big it might be flunked by the stewardess at the hatch door? And moreover, getting out of line—and going back to sit down—might well attract the actual, the full-blown, the non-imaginary heart attack.

Staying in line turned out to be the right thing. He'd made it to this minute without ruining the trip. His daughter was onstage, singing like a pro, standing up there in the furnace of light, making it look easy; she wouldn't have her debut wrecked by a father's medical complaint. She wouldn't have to find out till later. She would come offstage and only *then* have the little commotion in row 7 explained to her. The JumboTron projected her immense image behind her, along with her name, CARLOTTA PERDUE, sizzling and zooming onscreen. The air of the auditorium had somehow gone smoky, and laser-beam quills bristled from everywhere, seeming to originate in wildly swiveling projectors hidden in secret sockets all over the place. Different strobes kept photographing the multitudes' profiles and shadows. Onstage the band (the bullying, prodding horn section; the guitarists fronting their walls of amps; the mandarin drummer with his drum set staked out around him like a small village) was driving an avalanche behind his sixteen-year-old Lotta in her thrift shop red dress; she was so confident she never once checked behind herself; she kept them all at her back; she dipped her knees, like a surfer, and she poured her *whole head* backward, to *see* the note overhead at high noon, and she held the microphone up. It was the easiest song in her repertoire, "... *He's got the little bitty baby—in his hands. He's got the little bitty baby—*" She would sail through mistake-free. He'd heard her rehearse it a thousand times at home. And this weekend he'd seen the pro musicians nail it effortlessly. They would carry her past any glitches. But still a mistake onstage, even if only a perceived mistake, would cause a lot of grief, and she'd have to be talked down out of it. The fatherly necessity of keeping an eye on the rest of the performance: it's one of the reasons for a man's staying virtually, effectively, alive.

If this were a heart attack, at least he'd be going out of the world symmetrical, as always, heels together, knees together, elbows clamped to ribs, fingers tapping the armrests, four times each—*north south west east*—*north south west east*—forming that old prerational crux that absolves personal space. A heart attack felt statuesque. A heart attack didn't feel unjust, either. Society is naturally a competitive place, and at this point, at Berkeley, they had reduced him to a 2:3 schedule, including some undergraduate sections. People would say in his brief time Mark Perdue had made a great contribution to the field. They would also say I wonder who gets his office. For seventeen years he'd had the last door on the corridor, the double portion of windows, the old madrones outside, the remoteness from corridor hubbub. It was where he landed when he first came over and was considered to be a big hire. And realistically now, his death warrant in that place had been sealed on the day when he was standing by the faculty mailboxes and he overheard young Chaterjee say to young Nan Park, *We've got to keep Perdue out of Karlsruhe this year. He's dead weight. He's an embarrassment.* That such a thing was now sayable! It was almost a year ago, and its significance kept growing clearer and more logical, because in a big world-class physics department, any elderliness is quickly and efficiently punished; the pithing jab can be delivered right there easily, the faculty-mailbox room for an arena, delivered *accidentally* by a pair of newcomers like Chaterjee and Park. People had doubtless noticed and discussed his lapses into (Audrey's expression) "lymebrain"; like the lecture when, in front of a hundred students, he couldn't remember the atomic numbers of basic isotopes; and the department meeting where he temporarily *forgot* what the inverse-square law is, when somebody referred to it: everyone in the room could see, and the room got quiet; and the time he couldn't find his same-old usual parking place and was still wandering the campus as dusk came on, and *Dorothy* had to leave her desk and come out and lead him to it.

There was, too, the daily indulgence in Cafe Med's pastry, to be paid for at last. The pastries in the Med had a waxen sugar drizzle on top, which, over the years, will surely cement the arteries groping the heart's lower hemisphere, trying to provide oxygen to those muscles, those never-tired heart muscles, even during sleep, always knitting a fresh pulse. Called now by his own personal heart attack, he'd be able to *join* the fetus Noddy, in the glass fishbowl he imagined as a fetus's afterlife. Before they knew to abort it, he and Audrey made the mistake of giving it a cute temporary name of its own, and now three months later, the name kept lingering, the name alone, still out there, pecking and pecking at the outer cellophane-membrane of life, the little intergalactic shining cloud, the amniotic bag. Which, right now, estranged by his own chest pain, Mark was seeing through. What he saw, through the sac wall, was Lotta. She was onstage in the blaze of celebrity, holding a microphone, casually whipping the loose cord to unkink it. *She* at sixteen was so healthily seeking an independent life outside their three-bedroom condo that his influence as a "dad" would soon reach a natural tapering-off point, or had already reached it without his noticing. She'd be living in Connecticut in a few months. If she could figure out a way. Which she would. Being Lotta.

To be snuffed out, furthermore, by one economical little heart attack far from home would feel like justice because it would be punishment for a kind of infidelity this weekend. This weekend, he and their escort, Blythe, had fallen into a certain quiet understanding.

It was an understanding that could even arouse in the word *escort* its more unsavory meaning, something worth staying alive for, unsavory and actually reprehensible, for a man ten years older than Blythe, a man by comparison wise and cold. Over the days here, and the evenings, Blythe's green eyes had started to pull him down in, in the fathoms of their green, a green he'd underestimated at first. He might have felt some sort of a warning at the very outset in his own flinch of self-preservative aversion when he first saw her, in the L.A. airport holding up a MISS CARLOTTA PERDUE sign and wearing a kind of parody of chauffeur's livery, a man's blazer, too big for her, Charlie Chaplin-like, with the sleeves turned up.

Blythe, now, *she* would suffer if he were to keel over and die right here in the dark in the middle of the concert she'd so smoothly arranged. She would feel guilty. She would. She was a woman who took responsibility for all things, for everything everywhere, from Los Angeles's air pollution to an airline's baggage delay, or the lack of napkins at the fast-food place. She made it all her fault. If *he* now slumped over forward in an auditorium seat, it would be just one more thing. At this moment, she was standing at the side of the performance, watching from the shadows at a level below the stage—he could see her down there in the stage-manager's station—with her clipboard at her hip, her headphones' mic on its stem hovering at her lips, the Yankees ball cap on her head so she could keep a lid on her own beauty and not upstage the Celebrities.

His daughter, meanwhile, paced the parapet. That bright stage was the crucible of the future, and she was doing fine in it. She surely *would* find a way to escape home and get into a Connecticut school, and probably by next year she would be communicating with home only by emails and cell phone photos. In the airport on Friday, when he and Lotta, holding their boarding passes, were shuffling along in the queue through the old, dingy time machine tube toward the plane hatch, he'd been watching her shoulders in front of him, and they were unhappy shoulders, soft looking lately, rounded over in low expectations, and he was thinking how he'd never appreciated the strange life of women until he'd been a father of a daughter. All his life he had "cherished" women, or even in some way idolized them or just "wanted" them, they'd always seemed such alien creatures, differently evolved as slippery dolphins. And that form of devotion would always, no doubt perpetually, be available, to be drawn flashing from its scabbard but he hadn't known what a girl's graces were until Lotta, nor *felt* how *over years* his world was gradually changing shape so that females' natural secret regnant ascendancy became more impossible to ignore, not until Lotta, not until he'd started watching a girl take shape from earliest infancy, the fineness of discernment, as well as a soreness, which amounted to a discriminating kind of electromagnetic force, all superpowers in comparison with boys'—and how hard that all was for them, the amazing unremitting meanness of their competition, their fundamental sad practicality, then the encroaching ineluctable weird song and dance of their inferior competence.

Lotta was smart, and she knew perfectly well that the so-called Celebrity Vacation weekend in Los Angeles was devised to cheer *her* up because *everybody* was depressed about Noddy. The pinpoint hole left by that tiny subtraction was turning out to be a solid monument:

one of those monuments that, as it recedes in history, doesn't shrink, but swells, and gains a bulk and a gravitation in getting *farther* away. Lotta knew she was the family weather vane; it was her assigned job. And as a daughter she showed all diligence in undertaking that burden, the duty of being happy. Or at least seeming happy. Sad to see. The first onset of the lifelong loneliness. Which we all do vanish into. Even the trusting little girl with the shining eyes, even she will vanish into it, the universal business of being, or seeming, "happy." In the airplane line, standing behind her, he gave her carry-on a nudge with his toe and said, "Wanna trade? They'll reject this one of mine. It's too big."

She knew he was just razzing and flirting, and she didn't respond.

"They give beautiful girls a break. They're hard on sneaky old guys."

She sighed. She had detected the obtuse fatherly strategy to flatter.

"Ah, don't scoff. Don't scoff at the whole inevitable beauty problem," he said, while a kind of *hand* inside his chest was just slipping its first gentle but businesslike grip over his heart, the same hand that's holding the whole world, and the little-bitty-baby, and you-and-me-brother. "If you *got* beauty, you have to go along. And play along. It's still a sexist world out there, darling. *Your* generation might get things fair and square, but, still, you'll find everything is always gendered and sexual and sexist and sexy." He stopped there, having shocked himself, too, because it was true, the Freudian fact so large that he, for one, would never stand back and size it up.

She scorned to respond or even turn around. Instead she dove to unzip her carry-on and got out her little music player along with its skein of white wires for earphones. He had humiliated his teenager by talking audibly in the boarding queue, and in repentance he promised himself he would think before speaking, and censor all comments

9

except the necessary ones, from now on, throughout the weekend. Just to be in public proximity to a father is shaming. Lotta sometimes, in horror of his banality and gaucheness—or just anticipating it—held herself perfectly motionless, matching her background, the most delicate prey in the world. Her announced dread, this weekend, was that she wouldn't be talented enough to go on a "Fantasy Celebrity Vacation."

As she foresaw the advertised Three Days and Two Nights— recording session, video production, publicity party, stylist consultations, vocal coaching, limo cruise of Hollywood, gala music awards ceremony—she supposed that all the other children would have some special pizzazz and, furthermore, some kind of genuine, actual gift, along with the cunning and the social skills to display their gift to advantage. And Mark knew she might be exactly right. She might be entering in with a bunch of little egotist monsters. Who, however, would be very adroit little egotist monsters, succeeding well at the game. It was L.A. The whole thing could be an environment *crueler* than those high school corridors. But the brochure literature had been emphatic, in particular about the staff's care for everyone equally, in the nurturance of self-esteem *irrespective of any natural inequities in perceived talent*, as the Fantasy Vacations rep said in their first phone call. And she added, *Self-esteem for young people is Fantasy Vacations' stock-in-trade. We're very mindful of making the whole experience "Not About Winning-or-Losing."*

After they'd located their side-by-side seats on the plane, Lotta had pulled out the *SkyMall* catalogue and started flipping through it: *whack whack whack*. Then she tossed her hair—always the Lotta prelude to an utterance—and, referring to the fact that this was her mother's first day on a Habitat for Humanity job site, she drawled, *"Mom* sure looked cute in her carpenters' pants," with an actual sneer. The sneer had been appearing only recently in this sophomore time of life, a time requiring so much bravery, so much baseless faith. Absolutely baseless faith. There's no reason for hope during adolescence. When he was that age it looked to him like the girls were perfect and had everything easy. Lotta was pretty but she was not one of the popular kids, and the principle spur for this "Celebrity Vacation" experiment was that she'd started, during these last months of her sophomore year, to toss off snide little jokes about killing herself and about certain sex acts the girls in her class have picturesque new names for. As if they knew anything about it. And then there was her getaway plan. It started by her saying that they ought to move out of Marin County. When asked where they might go, she responded, "Iceland is supposed to be good." This in total seriousness. She'd heard great things about Iceland. "Or anyplace rural." Then she got in touch with her cousins in Connecticut and began talking about boarding school and, *on her own initiative*, sending away for application materials. So there. It seemed clear—in her silences, and her absences from rooms, in her ardent deadpan relief when making an exit of any kind, in her practice of secrecy in sending out boarding school applications—that the time had come for her to seek the world. If not this one Connecticut boarding school, then some other.

The particular comment on her mother's work pants was intended as an offer of peacemaking. During the drive to the airport in the cab, she had been making sarcastic, unnecessarily cruel observations about her mother. About her mother's looking like a homeless person during an odd week or two, this spring, when she was going out alone to pick up litter along the highwaysides of Marin, for miles, for whole afternoons, pretending it was a public-spirited environmentalism rather than simply a disguise of maimed grief—a solitary pastime, which fortunately ceased when the rainy season came back, and a pastime that probably would not return anymore, now that she'd hooked up with Habitat for Humanity. Father and daughter, both, were ambivalent about a middle-aged mom's ambition to apprentice as a carpenter. It was a program called Women Build. Audrey used to be a lawyer, right up until the maternity leave. Right up until maternity leave, she'd worn heels every day. She'd carried a four-hundred-dollar briefcase, and she'd billed for her time in six-minute intervals. Six minutes of her time was worth so much, it was funny around the house. Now she had a tool belt. It was a red, tough, nylon-web tool belt, and, wearing it, she walked out through the doorframe stubbier in stature, without the heels. Habitat for Humanity seemed an implausible adaptation but a development to be treated with patience, because of course it had to do with the fetus. Everything did. They should never have given it that name, nor should they ever have watched its early sonogram movies, in their little family screening with popcorn they called the NodFest.

Lotta, for her part, pretended to be particularly intolerant of a mother's going into construction. She'd been judging the world lately through the eyes of her girlfriend peers at school. And that gang seemed strict in their pragmatic "crush-the-weak" ethic. Lotta was doing her best to show no mercy, not anywhere. Having ridiculed her mother's pants, she went on slapping through the pages of the *SkyMall* magazine, not stopping to actually focus on anything illustrated there. (That one remark about her mom's carpenters' pants was a risky-enough sally into new dialogue.)

Mark, meanwhile, had been doing his usual reconnaissance of his airplane seat, its furnishings, his home away from home. Airplane seats in general he found to be blessedly symmetrical environments, but there were always a few stubborn built-in asymmetries: the welded-shut chrome ashtray in the armrest because this particular plane was a retrofitted 727; the hole for plugging in a headset; the germy tray table latch tilted like a big accent mark; the elastic pouch of desolate magazines with articles comparing restaurants in major cities, describing visits to spas, evaluating the shopping experiences in resorts. Are those—spas and shopping?—reasons for some human beings' staying, ostensibly, "alive"? Apparently, yes. But Mark, being honest with himself, wasn't a snob. He knew his own reasons weren't much more exalted. Particularly lately. He arranged himself in the Southwest Airlines seat. Over the years he'd more and more succumbed to his phobic dislike of touching airline magazines, gummy from many human handlings, which would stay eight inches from his knees during the forty-minute flight.

Because the tray table latch stood at a careless slant, he adjusted it by tapping with his knuckle until it was vertical, an exclamation point.

Anyway, as to Lotta's opinion that mom looked cute in her carpenters' pants, he replied, "She did. Yes. With her little tool belt."

In fact, Audrey looked great—she'd looked exactly like herself—and all over again he was grateful for her, for the organism there, the whole mystery there, the built-in good luck there, even during this recent period, when patience was called for. The new tool belt from True Value was red, redder than any valentine, its tough nylon webbing lustrous with that almost-lanolin stuff that synthetic hardware-store fabrics have when they're brand-new and still faintly cense the factory warehouse perfumes of polymerized thermo-plastic. The way it was slung, the whole belt had a way of locating her hips in the baggy jeans, discovering there a woman-shape. So far, the only tool she'd acquired to hang on it was the wooden-handled hammer from the

Tupperware box in the carport. It hung in its metal holster clip, dragging the belt at a rakish slant. She declared this morning (standing over them at the breakfast table, tall at that moment, having recovered a little of her old loft from the new heavy-soled work boots), "I have to be in Oakland in half an hour." Meaning this breakfast would be their good-bye. It would be a four-day separation. At the moment when their plane was lifting off the ground, she would be standing out in the Oakland sun on a fresh-poured concrete foundation, holding the old wooden-handled hammer from the carport. It was her first day, but she and the other trainees were being asked to "hit the ground running" (now, in the building trades, apparently everyone was going to talk like infantry). This particular project in Oakland was supposed to be a kind of publicity showpiece: in the short time of a three-day weekend, a gang of beginners would build six semidetached low-income homes, start to finish, under the direction of Women Build.

"They'll all be dykes," grumbled Lotta at the breakfast table, not lifting her eyes from the *Times* "Arts" page, her mouth full of cottage cheese and cantaloupe. These days she was testing out a new cynical sophistication in all directions at once.

Audrey only answered, "So, sweetie, I won't see you till you get back Monday night." She applied the kiss on the cheek. "Take care of your dad. Don't let *him* get up onstage. And hey," with a little punch in Lotta's direction, "knock 'em dead." (That benediction caused, visible to a father's watchful eye, an inward wringing.)

Lotta, though, at this moment onstage, was in heaven. The band, predictably, at this point did the key-change thing and lifted the whole tune a notch higher. She was coming into the home stretch. "*He's got you and me, brother—in his hands.*" Several video cameras around the (honestly rather small) auditorium were recording this for posterity, and the onstage camera had slid in, very close, a little rudely, though Lotta seemed not to notice. It crept on its big-wheeled dolly at a level beneath her, so she would appear in perspective to tower above it.

The man at the sound console below the stage was conferring with Blythe in her cute baseball cap: he seemed to adjust a knob—probably adding pitch correction—so Mark had been right in thinking that, maybe, in the last verse Lotta had hit a flat note. But Lotta didn't seem to have noticed. And this audience wasn't going to be supercritical; they were a crowd of random draftees who had shown up only because they'd accepted a handbill this afternoon on the L.A. sidewalks, inviting them to a free concert so they could form the necessary witnessing throng, a motley assemblage of shills, tourists, high school kids out for an idle thrill, bored cheap cityfolk happy to be anywhere—and of course other Celebrity parents, relatives, friends on the so-called guest list.

She threw out her arms, cruciform, and the song was over, mistake-free, it was a triumph, the drummer collapsed upon his last big rolling catastrophe at the foot of the avalanche they'd made. The teenager in her red dress, who had been so cynical and despairing about the fakery of a Fantasy Vacation, was standing onstage uplifted on a surging froth. The glitter in her eye! It might almost be, but surely wasn't, a tear. Such a moment of victory rewrote the whole weekend, all its contrivances. Those now might have been actual publicity parties, with actual media cameras. It certainly was an actual limousine that met them at the L.A. airport, with a placard in the windshield reading MISS CARLOTTA PERDUE, a certain green-eyed Blythe Cress introducing herself as publicist and media escort, its backseat bar stocked with Mountain Dew and candy. At least for this moment, temporarily, everything pasteboard was redeemed, as good as genuine. Lotta hadn't believed in joy since she was a tiny scampering girl on the carpet and she'd screamed with delight at her monstrous hulking dad. Now again belief was lighting her up. How long would that last—five minutes?— an hour?—before she sank inward again. And began mistrusting everything again. The Fantasy Vacation brochure philosophy was that a sense of personal fulfillment and the habit of success and pride can be "rehearsed." Rehearsed presumably for later use, over the years. Presumably, "pride" and "personal fulfillment" are to become normal, habituated conditions in life. Mark of course had secret doubts, down there wadded in the darkness of seat GG in row 7. It was his personal wisdom—his kingly, endpoint knowledge (always to be kept strictly under wraps)—that "pride" and "personal fulfillment" are the mistakes that sooner or later will be punished; pride and fulfillment being poisons intoxicating only to the innocent. All of which is not to be mentioned to a sixteen-year-old Celebrity in her glory.

Blythe, by the sound booth, was removing the headset of stage manager, because the limelight would now be turned over to another Celebrity for *his* allotted eight minutes onstage—the paraplegic boy from Shaker Heights who could do such a great drum solo. So at this point, *his* escort would take over as stage manager. And put on the headset. The cheers of the crowd were loud and apparently sincere, if padded somewhat in the PA system by a supplementary recording of a stadium crowd; it was an effect they added so lightly he wouldn't have noticed it if Blythe hadn't told him.

Blythe—her chipmunk face (yes, *chipmunk*! She was *his* chipmunk, his love and lifemate for just one weekend, and *chipmunk* captured her, her succinctly pursed cheeks, her provident, darting thrust, the complexion that looked freckly without having actual distinct freckles)—hopped the velvet rope and plopped down in the seat next

16

to him. Never to brush forearms. Never to exchange a knowing glance. They were always extremely careful. But at this moment they were in the dark in row 7. She said, "Well, now Lotta's headed for the green-room. They'll all be in there, living it up. She was great. I've seen this before. They do forget themselves, for about a minute."

She was only, loyally, endorsing the Celebrity Vacations philosophy. Mark was looking up into the rectangle of light, watching the crew who were breaking down Lotta's stage and setting up for the young drummer. He nodded toward the drum set as it took shape, and he told Blythe, "Those two last night didn't come home until about two in the morning."

Lotta and the paraplegic drummer had stayed downstairs in the hotel bar, drinking decaffeinated confections, communing, talking with bowed heads together. Mark had actually crept down, via elevator, about one in the morning to check on them, and they were consulting in such serious attitudes together they might have been praying, the boy's sporty no-armrest wheelchair docked at the table corner nearest Lotta. They had to be talking about Noddy. Just from how they sat, he knew. He could tell the Ohio boy was dispensing some kind of solace, or some kind of advice, and Lotta was being filled up by it. For some reason the relationship of supplicant to authority looked, to his fatherly eye, unwholesome, or fraudulent. They sat at a dim booth—the table's lightbulb was quenched—because the boy had environmentalist objections to the burning of electricity and made a point of turning out lights around himself, creating fresh darkness wherever he went.

Then later, after he'd gone back up to his bed, Lotta came up and let herself into Mark's room. Believing he was asleep, she sat for a few minutes on the arm of a chair, looking out the window into the warm haze of the L.A. night, then went off for her own room, closing Mark's door after herself with the saddest tact. It was as if she'd wanted to talk but lost courage. That boy had planted something.

Speaking of the drum set taking shape onstage, he grumbled to Blythe, "I suppose he'll sing 'I Am the Sun and the Moon and the Stars.'" It was the one he'd been rehearsing all weekend, an original composition.

Blythe only made one of her little eyebrow shrugs. With discretion. Because after all, she worked for Fantasy Vacations.

"So what happens to us?" Mark said, turning now to bigger things.

He did not want to have an affair. Nor did she. That was a basic, well-presumed axiom between them. Burnishing that axiom, he frequently brought up Audrey back home. And Blythe had some kind of boyfriend, named Rod, whom she'd mentioned as early on and as often as possible. "Rod" owned a used-record store. And he played the pedal steel guitar. So a whiff of marijuana or something came off of "Rod"—though not off of Blythe, curiously. Or, if not marijuana, just a shared dedication to a low-goal life. The whole setup made an affair unthinkable, fortunately. From the moment in the L.A. airport when they met and were, mutually, a little uncomfortable—and then later when they'd spied each other fatally across the room at the kids' meet-and-greet and been unable to tear their eyes away from each other—they'd known in their hearts right away that they were in trouble but, also, that in their separate lives, they were permanently planted at some crucial distance from each other.

The secret of Blythe Cress's power and allure here in this place, in her life, was that she didn't want anything—and had never wanted anything—but by a trick of lowering all standards and expectations, she had stayed inert in the world and after college she'd gone basically nowhere. Maybe Mark wanted to *visit that*—visit not-wanting-anything—because it seemed not only to have infinite eroticism in it, but it seemed, too, a kind of wisdom. He had surely married Audrey in his twenties because of all her wonderful qualities: Audrey was always beautiful, there was always that, more beautiful according to the conventional scorecard than of course he'd ever merited; she far outclassed him in poise and social skill, she was smart, she was enterprising in sex, she was honest, dependable; she had an income of her own; and the practice of the law was something he found interesting. Audrey had a lot of qualities back then—she still did today! all the more!—but this Blythe in L.A., she didn't need assets or qualities, there was something else, more important than qualities. Maybe the mysterious something goes under the name *vitality*. Yet it also went under the name *inertia*. Or *repose*. Whatever it was, she had it. They fit like puzzle pieces. This was unlike anything. And they both knew it. They both knew the whole situation was doomed and unlucky, while it was lucky all the same.

She said, "Los Angeles is a nightlife town. But—" She shed from her shoulders the idea of nightlife, born-and-bred Los Angelena, indifferent to the city's glamour. A girl whose parents three decades ago had had the wit to name their baby Blythe, she was now a grown woman to whom nothing mattered. Back home in Terra Linda, everything *mattered* so much, and everything was so consequential. Here a life with Blythe Cress would have been inconsequential—to the point of anonymity—a prospect that was even sexually nettling.

"Lotta did well," Mark said, not wanting to address too greedily the idea of going out on the town—then he asked anyway, "But what about Rod?"

The mention of Rod made her move her attention away, back to the stage. The special high-tech drum set up there was gradually shaping up. It looked like a space colony.

"He can be happy with his guitar friends. So we can do whatever. I frankly like just doing nothing. Like just dinner. I know a place. Media escorts know all the places." They'd trained their eyes parallel, watching the stage, avoiding the problem of their gazes' meeting. The wheelchair boy's drum set onstage didn't have actual drums; it was an electronic sort, with charged sensitive platters floating where drumheads would be. Meanwhile, Mark was scanning himself and finding that between him and Blythe there was, at bottom, a kind of shame, but it was an ashamedness only *he* was aware of. It actually pained him. For a minute, earlier, when they'd held each other's eyes, he'd had a sense that he was watching her through a mask. Because he was, yes, ten years older. And there *was* that mask. It was sleazy, this perspective.

Because maybe that was, obviously, no "heart attack" back there, but the truth was, those were ten important years intervening between them. And at her age, she had no idea. He was already coming into death compared to her, in the sense of being already philosophical, or already somehow cold—this was surely something the experience of Noddy had done. Whatever the causes, he was further on into the cold than she, further on into reality, and he wanted to stay married, in the way of the chastened, he wanted to "drink life deep" and all that. He wanted to apply himself in earnest to "the business of being or seeming happy." It was death coming; it was that medicine. Philosophy ran in his veins now; that's what she didn't know and didn't have any idea of. She was still warm and responsive, only ten years back. And so, it was as if he had somehow merely "retained" this woman, for a weekend while he was a visitor in town, so she might display the appearances for him, the appearances of the old delusions, of life and clinging. It was unfair to *her*, in a way defiling, that she should be viewed, unbeknownst to her, through this cool philosophical night-vision scope of his: her luminous, dancing, warm aura. For "an older man" or a man already getting acquainted with wisdom and the cold, there are going to be these shabbier, more vicarious relationships.

She added, still watching the stage crew, "Lotta will be fine. The chaperones are with them, and they get their limo tour after this. We could leave *now*. They've got the whole backstage scene. They have to have *their* little orgy. All the energy drinks and pizza they could possibly want."

★ CANDLE FLAMES STANDING steady in the balmy night of a Santa Monica terrace. White vertical flags of fabric, hung by interior decorators. Soundless, unnoticeable waiters. They had driven to a new restaurant in a hotel she knew about, because media escorts know all the places. And while they had a white wine and poked at little stunted vegetables on saucers, he undertook to tell the short, sad story of "Nod," to satisfy her curiosity. Gratifying people's natural inquisitiveness tended to be an unavoidable social duty. His own aim was always, via pious truisms and clichés' dead ends, to shut down a topic that was both tiresome and objectively trivial. Noddy was an event that would be mostly insignificant, from any *objective* spiritual point of view, if it hadn't been a traumatic ordeal for Audrey. And aggrieved his daughter.

He surprised himself, though, by beginning in an odd new place, with a certain irrational, dreamy part of the story, a certain fanciful, irrelevant perception he'd had during the pregnancy time—which he hadn't mentioned to anyone, nor even quite realized he'd *had* at the time—that in all the later sonograms, the image of the boy's head was a jack-o'-lantern.

Picturing that, Blythe's very young-looking face paused in a paralysis of polite tact, pending further info.

Whenever people wanted to commiserate over the abortion, Mark found himself in a deceitful position. He'd never been as saddened over Noddy as people's appetites required. The little iconic person they'd ensleeved with a temporary name had *gone from dark to dark* (a traditional Japanese expression for fetal death he'd seen on one of the many websites devoted to abortion grief, where people "blog" about their woes and quote the wisdom of prayer and pop songs and favorite poems and recommend books on recovery to each other, or religious anodynes, or homely remedies like chamomile tea or massages or shopping sprees)—he had "gone from dark to dark" in perfect isolation. In almost perfect inconsequentiality. As far as any *mourning* for that little *person* was concerned, a terminated embryo was a proverbial tree falling unwitnessed in the woods. But crowds of sympathizers seemed to have plenty of metaphysical ideas to wreak upon the Perdue family, as well as supernatural ideas, and morally apologetic ideas.

Mark could be sad for her sake, Audrey's sake; she was different; she'd been badly hurt. For her, it was a *bodily* jolt. The occult reproductive system—that sovereign brain, which nests in the pelvic basin, symmetrical as a Rorschach blot, dominant as an astrological constellation, ruling from the remote evolutionary past—had suffered a terrible insult: the actual *erasure* of its sketch for a human; and in vengeance it had churned up around Audrey an emotional weather system. Which she couldn't escape. Which she was still today navigating out of—hammer in hand, heading off for Oakland in the sunshine. An irreproachable, unassailable femaleness was in such grief. Mark, for himself, kept coming back to the fact that the organism had never been a consciousness or a person; but such a rationalism wasn't socially acceptable. It was actually impolite. Everybody had attitudes, and everybody needed to experience their own compassion, and curiosity too, like Blythe right now, by candlelight. So this would continue to be his social job, whenever it came up, to confess a decent wretchedness over the abortion.

Blythe, to frame an inquiry about the jack-o'-lantern in the womb, had lifted her hands to form a sphere around her own head, wincing inside that pumpkin.

"No," he said, "did you ever see a sonogram?" He set out to describe this funny impression he'd never explored much until now: the jack-o'-lantern wasn't the fetus's face; the actual face, naturally, appeared as the typical mask all fetuses display in a sonogram's black blizzard, the cute little pointy-nosed salamander, surfacing. They'd seen the same salamander sixteen years earlier in Lotta's sonograms.

The jack-o'-lantern image, rather, was formed by a slice through the top of the fetal skull, the cross-section oval of the cranium, showing where the boy's identifiable syndrome was visible. The pumpkin's "grin," then, was made by a black crescent at the lower rim. It indicated an empty area. It wasn't supposed to be there. And the jack-o'-lantern "nose" was a perfectly triangular absence at the brain's center, as a pumpkin might be incised with a kitchen knife. A fluid was collecting there, indicating a hydrocephalic condition. The corpus callosum was developing wrongly. If he'd had to pick out the "eyes," they would have been a pair of blurred watermelon-seed dots, small, close together, high in the oval, making this jack-o'-lantern a cretinous-looking one, but a jolly one.

That was the only way they ever said hello to the accumulating boy with the temporary name: by peering through the sonogram's apron-shaped window of night in a black snow of static, the Halloween grin in the white ring of bone when the fetus bowed his skull forward, the twiggy forearms and shins all folded together inside his big yolk, and on the ends of his wrists the bones of human fingers fine as bristles. The boy's actual little humanoid face, with its eyelids closed in patience, whenever it surfaced, was mysterious, tolerant, in its nirvana not the least bit judgmental, even slightly amused looking, so that you could almost see an incipient sense of humor. Such character traits—irony, mellowness—are indeed built into the bodily constitution, right into the bones and hormones and neurochemical paths. And traits like irony and a little tolerance would have served the boy well if he'd been born, born normal—and received a genuine name and grown up and (this was how Mark pictured the unlived life) had had a quiet existence in a white farmhouse somewhere. That was what he pictured. A little farmhouse, the kind of place where not much ever happens. There, a creature with all its faculties and the usual mellow equanimity could have *kept* its nirvana and never quite wakened. Like anybody. Like him, too. Like everybody, wading numb through the blaze.

But one thing Mark wanted to emphasize for Blythe. Lotta had been included in all the discussions. They'd agreed she was old enough and it would have been wrong to exclude her. And at the time she had no objections. She was decidedly in favor of the abortion of her little sibling, and in fact Lotta's ethical equipment was somewhat simplistic: all she could see was that (a) a woman has a right to choose, and (b) the child would have had a short, unhappy life. Those rubrics were enough for her. They were enough for Mark, too. And for Audrey. Maybe they were simplistic, but they were the truth. The particular syndrome (identified medically by a pair of hyphen-joined surnames, perhaps the names of the doctors who'd first identified the syndrome, a hyphenated formula too electrifying ever to speak aloud, the hocus-pocus that was the curse) was described in medical literature in bleak detail. A child with this affliction never lives past the age of ten. And during that decade he would have been motionless in paralysis, and in an unlifting mental fog, all his life. The issues were clear; nobody had any moral confusion over the thing. Least of all Lotta.

But then within a month, she started changing her story. She began claiming she'd said many times she would have been willing to quit school, in order to stay home and devote herself to caring for "Noddy," setting loose again the accidental *name* that had been sealed away permanently in its columbarium niche. It was pointed out to her that, if she ever really *had* said such a thing, she would have been talking about a ten-year commitment, ten years of standing by, to change his IV drip and mop his drool from his neck (if indeed he was lucky enough to retain the salivation capacity), ten years of diaper changing, ten years of reading nursery rhymes aloud to a little icon in a crib, in the pretense that it might do something helpful for him. Who would have been blind from the start. Who would have never seen the mobile suspended over him. Who was destined to die of pneumonia, or kidney failure, or heart malfunction, or something awful like bedsore septicemia, any number of things. Lotta, to all this, replied it would have been a decade well spent.

Throughout the story of Noddy, Blythe left her wine untouched but listened with her chin on her hand, her eyes unwavering. Then at last—after Mark fell silent and shrugged—she said, "I Googled you," and lifted her glass.

Mark took a sip of his own wine, which tasted all right to him. He'd lived in California almost twenty years but would never understand the wine thing. Whereas Blythe was sophisticated about it. It mattered to her, what she was drinking. After a certain hour of every day this long weekend, an uncorked bottle was always a lamp at her elbow, or somewhere nearby working its magic. He sighed, changing gears, moving away from the great Nod singularity, happy to do so—but not happy to move on to a discussion of his little one-time fame as a physicist. It would be hard to explain his ambivalence now about the period of his life when he had a popular book out. He'd never exactly lived that down among his colleagues. And in recent years, since he'd started having undisguisable "lymebrain" mental lapses publicly, it seemed all the more absurd: how arbitrary were the choices of the vulture of good fortune, who had come down and closed its talons on *him* at age twenty-two and then quickly dropped him.

She was swirling her wineglass, its hoop below her face. "*And* I YouTubed you. Old *Nova* episodes are on. The great Mark Perdue explaining physics. Looking young!" Yes, he remembered perfectly and with remorse. The *Nova* producers had thought they were being witty when they stood him up on-camera in front of a lightning bolt made from a zigzag of cardboard covered in aluminum foil. And they'd dressed him up in a wizard's gown printed with stars and moons, holding a wand tipped with an aluminum-foil star. All because his dissertation seemed to imply that science had gone metaphysical.

He glanced around the restaurant, rescued by the future here. He always said he disliked Los Angeles, but really he'd only disliked the *idea* of Los Angeles that exists in one's mind. In fact, this was nice. Every place is nice if you get to know it. If you discover its tendernesses. If you just simply get off the freeway.

"Your wife is surely not over it? I mean Audrey? Over the loss of Nod?"

So the subject would revert. Blythe was so extremely considerate she was able to *seem* as if she were cheerfully insensitive but meanwhile maneuver among his many sore spots—the drama of his daughter, the Berkeley job, the inconsolable wife, his run-in with Lyme disease and evidence of decaying mental powers. Everything with Blythe was in some sense *her* responsibility, her care, her purview, and she kept her stitches invisible, on the fabric's "wrong" side, as seamstresses say.

"Audrey, yes. Audrey is devoting herself to charitable activities. You know, she used to be so 'important.' She, like, used to get her hair done on a twice-a-week basis and charge it to the office."

"Mm," said Blythe. "Lawyer."

"As I told you, she's doing the Women Build thing this weekend. You know they say—psychologists say—the principle symptom if you're close to somebody who dies, right off the bat, is guilt, for survivors. 'Inappropriate guilt,' they say survivors get. I told you about the period she was going out along the highways with trash bags picking up beer bottles, like sleepwalking."

"Well, I'll tell you, she sounds like a solid person," she said. She was seeing how truly lucky Mark indeed was. So there again was the agreement: no romance. Blythe refilled her own glass to near the brim. In ordering they'd asked for the complete megillah—a pasta course, a fish course, on and on, different wines—not because they were big gourmets, but because, without saying so aloud, they were colluding in making the dinner last as long as possible. (She'd said when they were ordering, "Nice thing about a hotel restaurant: they'll have a night staff. So you're not keeping some poor busboy from punching out and going home, if you, like, order a liqueur.")

"I just think it's so *interesting*," Mark said, "that she claims she would've quit high school to take care of her little invalid brother. Not that I'm interested in detecting 'hypocrisy' in a sixteen-year-old girl. It's just interesting how this moral idea—this atoning, self-sacrifice idea—came along. Like her mom picking up highway litter. And how now Lotta is being so nice to *him*," with a thumb over his shoulder.

29

"You mean nice to Bodie?" she said.

Bodie was the paraplegic drummer.

Mark was being unfair. The attentiveness to the disabled boy was more than charity. There was some kind of ardent admiration there. Sometimes, yes, he'd seen the dire glance of infatuation. The boy was— who knows?—perhaps impotent from the waist down, but from the waist up he was an Adonis, an athlete, with powerful arms and chiseled features, hair of gold, long and thick and wavy, and a cleft in his chin. He wrote his own songs, according to certain winning recipes. He sang about his ennobling environmentalist ideals, which were somehow avant-garde, and very strict, so that he turned off lights wherever he went, and he declined to take the "limo cruises" with the others and even chose his meals according to a personal menu that would conserve fossil fuels and protect animal species and preserve human rights worldwide. He was unfailingly polite among his inferiors the grownups, with all the discretion of his withheld power. When it was time for music, he would, with guiding biceps, glide on his wheels up to his space-age electronic drum set of levitating disks, set the wheelchair brakes hard with the heels of his palms, swing himself over onto his special drum throne, and pick up a pair of sticks and take real authority over the set. He *smiled* when he sang into the mic that poked at his face from its boom stand, smiled and closed his eyes; and when he sang, his already-thick neck got a lot thicker. The two kids' long séance together last night in the bar, over decaffeinated soymilk drinks, was a new, deeper step in an intensifying relationship—which had started when Lotta tagged along to his first recording session so she could loiter like a groupie in the control booth, watching. After that, too, on the Second-Day Excursion to see the sights of Hollywood, she opted instead to go out with Bodie, on foot, pushing his wheelchair along the desolate, thundering downtown boulevards, rather than going with the rest of the gang in the Celebrity stretch.

Mark said, "Maybe that will have been an unexpected dividend of the 'Fantasy Vacation.' Maybe Lotta is living out the fantasy of being a warm, loving person. Good fantasy to experiment with. We all ought to experiment with that one a little more."

Blythe made a smile, and looked down, and lightly petted the rim of her wineglass.

"Last night," he said, "they stayed down drinking desserty things till two in the morning. She *is* pretending to be 'in love,' I think."

He hadn't actually thought so, not in such unambiguous terms, not until just this minute. Using the word *love* made the idea real.

Blythe's facial expression, also, made it real—an expression (he associated it with therapists and shrinks) inviting further utterances while promising there would be no judgments, just an expectation that there might be a little more to say on the topic.

He said, "As you may know, Bodie is in trouble, over the long term, in some kind of awful way. Medically. Prognosis-wise. It's some kind of terminal condition he's got." (Though the boy certainly did look robust.)

Blythe was, still, giving him the therapist's nonjudgmental gaze.

"I just notice," he said. "Interesting correspondence. After Noddy was taken care of, well, this boy Bodie is like a reincarnation. Of the defective Noddy. One who was *not* aborted."

Blythe looked at him steadily, as if she were giving serious consideration to that insight. But she wasn't, because she said, "I ought to tell you something," and she leaned back and folded her arms. (They'd taken a table by the wall, and she was on the upholstered-bench side.) "Just while we're all recovering from something."

"I suppose *you've* got a terminal disease?" he joked. But it was a not-very-clever joke; it was a stupid joke, because what if she did have a terminal disease?

"No. Fortunately. What it is is . . . I didn't tell you this before. It's not the sort of thing you'd want to get into, right off. But my boyfriend? Rod? He's actually dead. He died recently. I've mentioned him as if he were still alive, because it's not—like—light conversation. But he died six months ago. So, you see, I have this thing of my own. Which I'm getting over. I'm rather close with Rod's *family*, so *that's* good." She scoped out the rest of the restaurant, its murmurous depths. Then she pulled her water glass closer and watched her fingers as they turned it on its axis, its wet crystal facets.

No boyfriend. In this news Mark discovered a nice unholy gladness. Because the gaudy jacket of death was around her too. Maybe he'd sensed it. Or even been drawn to it. The scummy green of her eyes. The first glimpse in the airport. People may know little about their own inner depths; but about each other, subconsciously everything; for people are at every instant photographing silhouettes of each other subliminally, far below conscious notice. Maybe it was during the first ride out of the airport in her limo—maybe it was something in the set of her shoulder, or a dental-office smell rising off her skin, the shallowness of her gaze, so maybe death was the perfume from the start, and maybe she, too, was on the brink of the philosophic chill, so their little love this weekend was not a "love" at all, but a camaraderie, in a kind of afterlife they were coexisting in.

"Of AIDS," she went on. "With mental complications. Dementia complications. He was loose on the street in the end. He loved escaping and getting out on the street and being homeless, so it was pretty terrible. We had to keep go-*finding* him. Now, I don't have AIDS. Or HIV. But he sure did. It went on for years."

As a first reaction, Mark came up with the response, "Wow," which of course was insufficient, but it was meant to be an open gate for more.

She said, "So I've got something, too, I'm dealing with." She smiled.

"You had to be a 'Selfless Person' for some while. Gee."

Her eyes glided away. "Yup. Selfless Person. For a while. And got the Inappropriate Survivor Guilt you mention."

"Well, Blythe, you. You feel guilty about everything. Leaving the *airport* on the 405, you were apologizing to us for other drivers' cheating in the carpool lanes."

How amazing. For a few years she'd been a "Selfless Person," as he'd phrased it.

He started organizing his place setting—centering his water glass, aligning it vertically with his wineglass, restoring the silverware to perpendicularity, sheathing the knife blade and the tines of his fork inside the linen napkin out of sight, the way he preferred, because it always felt like good luck, not to have sharp, shiny points exposed—then gripping the table edge symmetrically to left and right. Meanwhile he was getting Blythe Cress into a better focus. There was a life-arc developing here. She'd gone to art school; and all the while, her Rod was a musician, so she and Rod, when they were starting out, would have been an "artistic" young couple beginning a heedless, carefree, bohemian life together. Then would have come the symptoms, the medications, the unreasonableness of the patient, the chores for the caregiver.

He took up his own wine, while receding. She led a complicated life. The media-escort job, for her, was only a sideline. She'd said she'd gone to the Rhode Island School of Design. Her real career was as an antique appraiser at some auction-house establishment. She was an expert on old textiles from Asia, kimonos and samurai outfits. She'd said she did appraising in other departments too—cloisonné, netsuke, woodblock prints, exotic textiles. Supposedly it amounted to a part-time job, occupying a carrel of her own in a warehouse building on Sunset Boulevard; the place was called Gladstons, handling old weavings and garments, assigning minimum-bid estimates for auctions. Now, in addition, she'd had a crazed, deathly ill boyfriend living on the streets.

"What was Rod like?" Mark said.

"*Talented* pedal steel guitarist. He's on people's CDs. What he really was, though—I don't know if you've heard of Wrecked Records. It still is an L.A. institution. It started on Melrose, and then it moved and got bigger, and got other locations. Records and CDs and collectible vinyl. And some furniture? Like *sarcastic* furniture? So that was his real thing. But he caught the AIDS virus from needles. He once had a drug habit, back in the '90s. In the end he was very nasty and cantankerous and insisted on living outside and looking like a fucking *Lord-of-the-Rings* slimy *orc*,"—she could have almost giggled—she hadn't expected herself to say such a thing. All the while she was lifting her purse flap, taking out her wallet.

She opened the wallet bookwise to a photograph, and she revolved it 180 degrees and slid it across to him, still holding it down to keep it from springing shut, implying she would keep custody of it.

Rod—in better days—had long silky black hair with a wave at the end, and bangs cut straight across the forehead. It was a Prince Valiant style.

"He looks like Veronica Lake," he said, insensitively. "His hair does."

Unlike Veronica Lake, Rod had a small black goatee. He smiled broadly in the photo, as people did once in yearbook photos.

"Hm," said Blythe. "Except not blonde."

"Veronica Lake was brunette. Betty was the blonde." He was trying to remind her of the cartoon characters in the *Archie* comic books.

"Veronica Lake was a movie star."

"No, Veronica is Archie's girlfriend. She and Betty. In the comics." He had a general sense of losing traction, and he knew he shouldn't be insisting, but the resemblance was perfect. At least in the hair department, Rod did look exactly like the svelte brunette in the comic book. Rod even had the girl's heart-shaped face. Plus goatee.

"In the *Archie* comics, that was Veronica *Lodge*, not Lake. But you're right. Rod did have hair exactly like that."

"Veronica 'Lake,' Veronica 'Lodge,'" he flipped a hand. All the stars were always interchangeable. At least to him.

So, for a funereal moment, they were both looking at the image of a man no longer alive. All that remained was his picture in a wallet. And his historical resemblance to a comic book character. And the record store he'd founded. And the pedal steel playing that appears on people's CDs. Not a bad life. Blythe was folding her wallet and putting it away.

"Veronica in the comics was the bitchy one," she clarified. "With the little tycoon father. Betty was the blonde one. She was the 'nice' one."

A good-looking small platter arrived in the hands of a waiter. And a pair of ceramic mugs.

At that moment, a cell phone was chiming. It might have been coming from anywhere in the room, but it was, in fact, buried in Blythe's purse. "Uh-oh," she said, recognizing a ringtone, while she dug for it, "That's Billie at the office." She seemed puzzled as she examined her phone's incoming-call window. "Billie should be at home. Tonight's not her night."

Whatever this was, it could ruin their dinner. And he found he was—like a teenager—furious at any threat to his selfish plans. Earlier tonight, he'd been contemplating dying of a heart attack. Now he was a jealous, angry boy. Philosophy is only for the dying. Objectivity, stoic dispassion, "wisdom," all only for the dying.

Blythe said into the phone, "Well, when was the last time she was seen?"

Here was the nightmare that couldn't possibly happen, the disaster that could be forfended by, alone, carefree reckless ignorance. He watched her, while trying to summon a communicative look, but she kept her eyes down on the plate that had just arrived before her, little wafers of raw fish flesh fanned out.

"I see," she said at last, having done some listening. "He's here with me. We're at Avignon. All right."

She folded her phone and looked at Mark.

She told him, "I guess Lotta was upset."

"Was?"

If he *were* showing any anxiety, Blythe's hands were rising, patting, tamping down. "It's nothing awful, she's fine, she's great. We'd better go, though. Maybe we can get them to wrap this up. Take it with." She touched the midpoint of the tablecloth between them with a little tickle on the fabric and explained. "Lotta seems to have left the group. She *was* in Bodie's car." She lifted a shoulder. "But she got out of Bodie's car. She's on Sunset Boulevard somewhere."

Mark was getting out his credit card. "So it's a romantic snafu," he said. He pictured Bodie, planted deep in the car seat with his paralysis, yearning sidewise and trying to kiss Lotta, while Lotta squirmed and stiff-armed the poor fellow.

Blythe was pulling on her little jacket-thing. She cried, "Oh, too bad! And just when I wanted to ask you about physics and get an explanation *why* there's no such thing as a 'moment in time.' As you say repeatedly on YouTube."

FIRST, IN HER car, he did the obvious thing, he dialed Lotta's cell phone, but he knew what would happen. He of course got the recording of her voice (*Hi everybody, it's Carlotta. Leave me a message*)—but only after she'd let it ring six times—meaning she knew it was him but didn't want to answer. Blythe as she drove listened to the failure of the call. And when he folded his phone she told him, "The area where she got out, all along there it's safe. It's all tourists and shoppers. One of my, actually, favorite restaurants is there." She glanced to see if he was worried. "This happens often. Somebody goes off, and whenever it happens *Billie* has to come out—and she has to get *you* to come out—because legally now you're responsible for the little Celebrity, not Fantasy Vacations Incorporated. Billie will be there. She'll meet us at the Studio Lot, and then we'll look for Lotta. And just keep calling till she does answer. She's just riled up."

The story, as Blythe had got it from Billie, was that Lotta was spied in the back seat of Bodie's limousine, and that she wasn't resisting but rather taking an active part. They'd been parked in a side street. The two kids who had looked in through the tinted glass and, quite by accident, caught them were Rachel and Josh, a girl from New York and a boy from San Diego, a pair of teenage Celebrities on the tour who themselves had been developing their own romance during the weekend.

These, all of them, were all good-hearted kids; nobody was invidious in the way Mark had feared spoiled children would be, and nobody would want to embarrass Lotta. They tended to take care of each other. The New York girl, Rachel, had ambitions as a singer-songwriter and strummed an acoustic guitar while simultaneously managing the curtain of her lustrous hair, keeping it away from the guitar fretboard; and Josh was a very serious classical pianist who preferred to be called by an Arabic name: he was either pretending to convert, or had genuinely converted, to Islam (at age sixteen, from Mormon parents, in the pretty little Southern California town of La Jolla). Everyone kept reverting to calling him Josh, because the Arabic name he'd chosen was completely unmemorable; also, it involved a throat-clearing sound in the middle that nobody could master. He had made a minor nuisance of himself, during the week, by requiring that all his food be halal, somewhat overscrupulously halal, and complaining that the girl Celebrities in the group, including Lotta, dressed too revealingly and danced too suggestively. (However, he and Rachel were the only two kids on the trip who were known to be, at night, tiptoeing in the corridors visiting each other's rooms.)

For their tryst, Bodie and Lotta's limousine had been parked on a street off Sunset Boulevard. After their friends discovered them embracing, Bodie and Lotta had rapped on the screen that occludes the driver in the front seat, and they told him to get going. Then, after a few blocks, Lotta asked him to stop so she could be let off, apparently in some emotional distress. The driver was going to be reprimanded by the Fantasy Vacations office because it turns out the drivers are legally responsible for the return of their young Celebrities to their hotel rooms. He'd been sent straight back to the neighborhood, to have a look around for her, but of course Lotta had long since traveled up Sunset, and he'd had to report back that he couldn't find her. Mark, for his part, as father, would find the driver excusable, because he knew Lotta, and how ravishingly authoritative she could be (particularly when she was agitated).

The driver had told the chaperones, and word got out, and all the other young Celebrities learned that Lotta was out there alone somewhere, so they all began to fret over her. They saw her as a girl who didn't merely need to be located, she needed to be redeemed from a boy's infamous discourtesies. They all wanted to form a search party. She was out alone in Hollywood, standing on a curb somewhere, presumably wearing the same outfit she'd performed in, the red dress from the thrift shop. With a slit hem.

Her disabled boyfriend, meanwhile, had told the driver to take him back to the hotel, where he had holed up in his room. Bodie was a young Celebrity who had come on the trip without his parents. This was his second year with Celebrity Vacations, and his parents had preferred to stay home in Shaker Heights. (The other orphan this week was Rachel. Her parents, too, had stayed home even though it was Rachel's first time, but Rachel was such a sophisticate she could go anywhere.)

Mark, looking within himself, found that there were *layers*. A topmost layer of him absolutely forgave both kids of course; a little misjudgment in love is a trifling and even necessary learning experience; he had once been young, too, and he knew all about the vagaries of flirting, delight, acquiescence, mistakenness, and he was even slightly pleased, that Lotta should have the blessing of ardors. All this is part of life. Looking at the thing in this light, he hated it that, through bad luck, her first foray into that enchanted forest had become a public comedy. Yet another part of his mind kept reverting to the scene itself.

41

Since Bodie was paralyzed from the waist down, and since there was the added pathos of his terminal illness, he had to wonder. What were the emotional assumptions in this relationship—and what were the mechanics, too, incidentally?—because the terrible picture to be blackened from imagination was of Bodie's handsome lip snarling in sedentary lordship's pleasure. There was a certain paternal layer of himself that sent wrath surging into his hands. He sat there in the zipping, lurching Subaru watching the strip malls of L.A. go past—all looking universally like crime-scene footage from the ten o'clock news—and he despised the suave expression he imagined on that Bodie's handsome face. Disability or no disability, Bodie was an operator. There was, in Bodie's perfect courtesy and self-assurance, something authoritarian, something fascist; it was visible even at the first day's Meet-and-Greet, a vigilance, a hyperalertness. The boy had a way of seeming, though seated, to tower over others in the room.

"Does that one, in fact, *have* a terminal condition?" he snapped, recklessly. He hadn't really considered anybody could doubt Bodie's claim to be doomed. There was no empirical reason to disbelieve him.

However, his intuition seemed right on target because Blythe, while she drove, rolled her eyes and let out a deflating whistle. For a minute she paid attention to driving, and then she admitted, "On the one hand, I personally believe him, but his medical form they fill out mentions nothing terminal. And some people on staff have noticed how he tends to *tell* people all about it, when he first *meets* people. But personally I wonder why would anybody want to invent such a story?"

Mark imagined the boy now back in his hotel room raiding the minibar for all its chocolate, by way of solace. Calling up room service. Watching television on the bed. Doing the daily calisthenics that keep him in such tip-top shape.

Right now as father it was his main job to protect and salvage Lotta's fragile dignity. Without censoriousness, without making evaluations, nor even inquiring into the facts, the thing to do would be to find her and get her out of the environment of Celebrity Vacations— and if possible transport her away, to some distraction. If she were still five years old, an ice cream cone would make everything all right.

His own cell phone started ringing. It wouldn't be her, it would be Audrey at home. It was the home ringtone, and this was the right time of the evening for her call.

So HE PULLED it out. Now was as good as any other time. Also, if he didn't answer, Audrey would think it strange.

At the same moment, Blythe's phone began clanging—probably her boss Billie again—so she groped over the dashboard for it.

"Hi," said his wife. He could tell right away Habitat for Humanity had, again today, done nothing to lift the long discouragement. According to her accounts so far, she wasn't sociable on the job site among the other women. She didn't even take lunch breaks but just kept on working alone during the noon hour, while presumably sandwiches were broken open and Thermoses passed around in some nearby shade among "all the guys." For them it must be like having a zombie on the crew, in the noonday sun the suburban blonde walking around the concrete-pad foundation, carrying her heavy nail gun, firing spikes into studs and floor plates, while others ate.

"How'd it go? Did they give you any more tools, sweetie? For your poor little tool belt?"

He told her the show was perfect and Lotta had been great and she'd brought down the house. None of this was being overheard by his L.A. girlfriend, here, because she was on her own phone. And all of it was perfectly true.

Clearly some amount of duplicity would be called for. Also, this *separate* problem was *not* in any way connected with his own little swoon of infidelity this weekend, his being so enchanted with Blythe that his arms and chest sometimes went all concave, bowl-like, with his not embracing her.

"She did 'Whole World in His Hands.' She didn't miss a note. She looked great. There was a big audience, too. They got all these *people* and the mock-up of a real concert was so realistic *I* got excited. I felt myself in the presence of an entertainment idol."

"Was there one of those dancing melee things and you jumped in?"

"The interesting thing was, Lotta had of course been sarcastic as hell. You know how she is. She's been a pain all weekend. She's got a put-down for everything. And how phony everything is. But then tonight? Tonight she believed it. She actually believed." (Out of nowhere, he had a lump in his throat, the onset of the common, ridiculous grief of a father, seeing the day she'll go to Connecticut and seldom call anymore.) "Tonight she had a light in her eye."

"Well, all right. I guess it's a good thing then," she said. *She* had come to be the more skeptical, dubious one, in the back-and-forth discussions about whether to spend the *five thousand dollars* on a Fantasy Vacation package, whereas Mark had increasingly found himself taking the less skeptical position, in a departure from habit, *endorsing* this "adventure in self-aggrandizement" as Lotta herself had been calling it.

"Right at this moment I'm being taken back to the hotel," he lied adulterously to his wife—with not a glance at Blythe, who wasn't listening anyway because she was having her own phone conversation on her own little hinged phone. "I've had dinner. And the kids are out doing the limousine cruise together."

"How did the other kids do? Did the paraplegic drummer have a good experience?" There were altogether seven teenagers, and Mark had been keeping his wife up to date on the several interesting personalities.

"Bodie. Yes, he brought down the house. They all bring down the house, it's guaranteed. The New York girl Rachel was good, she sang one of her protest songs. Her performance is about her hair, how it's falling over the guitar frets, or *not* falling over the guitar frets. As I've told you, she has amazingly pretty hair. Now *she's* made a kind of boyfriend of that boy Josh. And he did well. Josh is the classical one. He was great. And David? From Chicago? He's the gay one?"

"My wrist is weird. I was Lady Nail Gun again today." He loved— he was always cheered and fortified by—his wife's non sequiturs. She had, by this time of the evening, granted herself the nightly indulgence of a single glass of Guinness, the black beer with the tan suds. She sounded at this point about halfway into it, at the mellow middling spot in the evening when the TV commercials, like clockwork, trend toward insurance ads, investment ads, erectile dysfunction ads, calcium bone-loss ads, an autumnal harvest of anxieties and debilities for all. He wished he were beside her, TV clicker in hand, side-by-side sailing into that obscurity together over the years. "We got all six units now with rough plumbing and insulation and half the Sheetrock. We're cheating a bit, because work has been going on already in preparation: they wanted to make a big spectacle in time for Earth Day. It's why the foundations were prepoured, and all the trusses and walls were stacked up, ready for us. The framing was all prefab tilt-up. Do you know what that is? 'Tilt-up'?"

"Oh my dear," said Mark. "You're a big construction worker now."

"Lotta was right about how many lesbians."

"Well," (he couldn't help but clarify, and Audrey was used to it, she was married to him) "the distribution would be a standard equation."

She sighed. He was right about the Guinness: she sipped it. "It's the East Bay. It's nice," she admitted gloomily. "All the little Rockridge places are catering our lunches." By this point in the evening, while the TV flickered before her eyes, she would be well sunken, deep into the pit of her inconsolable mysterious struggling, chafing, in her self-imposed quarantine, while Mark every night tended to just sit by uselessly like a lifeguard. Within an hour, it would be bedtime there, and she would tap the TV to kill it and leave it behind and go and put her glass upside down in the top rack, press the SMART WASH button on the face of the dishwasher, and go upstairs, consigning the kitchen to darkness, while the dishwasher began roaring and clinking by itself in the room.

She said, "But Mark?"

She was going to warn him again about her old father. This was the "father" tone. The topic had become an obsession.

"Dodd's people at Yew Garden haven't called lately, but he *is* just obnoxious."

The topic of Dodd seemed to come up once a day, as if for cyclical reasons of body chemistry. A husband had to listen and not contradict—nor even *agree* either, because agreeing, too, could come back at him as the insensitive thing to do. The Yew Garden, in Boston, was where Dodd lived, half blind now, demented, joyful, uncareful of his bowels, contemptuous of diapers, foxy, full of high spirits. She wanted him to come out and move into the spare bedroom. Which was not going to happen. Never. The only thing Mark had to do was keep listening and not replying. Dodd was happy at the Yew Garden, and the staff at the Yew Garden was well paid to take care of him.

Audrey said, "He may live another ten years, you know. He's healthy as a horse. And Mark, I really think, now that I've quit at Carson Carlin—"

"Can we discuss this another time?"

"I'm just saying. The poor staff at the Yew Garden just aren't equipped. I mean, for Dodd's kind of energy. He gets into everything. He's having the time of his life."

"But let's talk another time, Audrey. I'll call you tomorrow, is that all right?"

"You got a fax, from *Journal of Advanced Research*. It's the text of an article for the fall issue. They cite you and Martingger, and they need your approval. And you know, Mark? It's actually good."

"I don't want to see it. Just okay it for me, would you?" he said in misery. Of course the citation would be "good." It would even be patronizing.

"No, I mean they really get it. The whole article is good, and they credit you very nicely. You'll like it. It's not the usual thing."

"I'm exhausted," he told her, his voice tone a declaration of— if peeved—gratitude. But Audrey wouldn't hear that; she would only hear the peeved part. Blythe was finished with her own phone call, so now his so-called escort would be able to hear him lying to his wife. "Really. It's been a big day. And Lotta's fine. She and the kids are cruising up and down Sunset Boulevard as if they owned the town. Under the eagle eye of all their chaperones."

Audrey, anyway, was content to end the conversation, too. So they said their farewells. And when he'd gotten free and folded his phone and put it away in his jacket, Blythe told him, "We're supposed to meet them all. They're at a place on Sunset."

His call had ended with some intimate old closing endearments that nailed, once again, how make-believe was any idea that he and Blythe, in Los Angeles, had any kind of genuine relationship at all. He shifted and tossed in his car seat as if to suppress, to sit on, the embarrassment. The endearments had been uttered plainly in Blythe's hearing, just a pair of the usual married sweetnesses. In a way it was a good thing—it was worse than embarrassing; it was frankly degrading to Blythe as his temporary girlfriend—but it was a good thing if it set another seal on his faithfulness to his wife. Marriage was a dark little edifice unenterable by this girl. Mark Perdue and "Audrey Naale" (as she once was) had been wedded by their dark future, even from earliest days, back when the sparkle of innocence was on their gaze, dimming insight, like all mortals', for even the innocent are omniscient, as well as clairvoyant, though they censor it. Mark and Audrey in the depths of clairvoyance had been wedded by the sound of the dishwasher in the future, every night its rumble. Every night while they slept upstairs side by side at night, it did its work in the darkened kitchen, a kind of time-piece down there, clinking and churning away by itself, unobserved. Thus does "time" pass in other rooms, without *him* there to observe it: that's the implication, epistemologically. So much of the world transpires in one's absence. All the world, really. One ought to be used to that. It shouldn't feel like a surprise or an injustice. One's abiding *absence* from everything is a circumstance that he in particular, professionally, ought to have become comfortable with, rather than thinking of it as if it were some alarming new problem.

"So all the kids are *crazed* about this lovely *drama*," said Blythe as she swung through a left turn. In the aftermath of The Phone Call From The Wife she had a generous way of cutting straight for superficiality; she was so brave, alone now without Rod. Maybe even *with* her Rod friend she'd been alone, brave, cutting for the superficial. "They all want to go out in a posse, all over L.A., and look for her. We have to get them back to the hotel. But here's something. Bodie isn't in his hotel room. The front lobby security camera saw him leaving by himself."

"In his wheelchair?"

"Wheeling off into the night. Heading west on Wilshire toward La Brea. Twenty minutes ago."

"What were those two exactly . . . *doing* anyway?"

"Bodie and Lotta?"

His tone was sharp involuntarily. "In their little—back of their little—car."

Blythe stuck out her elbows and sped up, to cut through a yellow light at a corner, swinging left onto Sunset Boulevard—so they must be getting close.

"I mean, what exactly is the sin that was committed?" He shouldn't be curious about this aspect of it. He really didn't want to know and shouldn't have asked.

"Oh," she said, "just the usual thing I'm sure. Nobody mentions. She's just a little mortified. And all these kids, they're sweet, they're all embarrassed *for* Lotta. And *worried* about Lotta. They want to spread out over the city in their little dragnet. How's Audrey? I see the plan is, for the moment, not to tell Audrey anything. Until there's something to tell."

★ THE BASE COST of the Fantasy Vacation was five thousand, which was extravagant by Mark's and Audrey's standards, but they'd come into an inheritance in the past year, an inheritance that was large and peculiarly unasked-for. By a little heedless expenditure one might wash some excess good luck back out into the world. Mark wasn't the type to want a, say, red convertible or whatever affluence buys, a Harley-Davidson motorcycle, a lap pool, an esoteric voyage. They were all too busy with their chosen lives to embark on the kinds of things the middle-class rich do: take a barge up the Seine, etc. And they didn't want to move. To where? Belvedere or Ross? The new money was probably just enough to buy one of those big places in Ross but, then, not enough to maintain it. Plenty of Cal professors might want to move to the East Bay hills. But Terra Linda was convenient, the freeway was right there, it wasn't fashionable, but it was home.

And the new money had unhappy origins and associations. The first news of it happened to arrive on the day, more than a year ago, when the three of them—Audrey, Mark, and Lotta—had cracked open the initial discussion, about whether or not a little sibling would be nice to have, as an addition to the family. In a lunchtime conversation the three of them all more or less agreed how much fun—and for Lotta, how much daunting responsibility!—a baby would be. Lotta, who was fourteen then, particularly wanted a boy, a brother, and she said she was casting a magical spell on her parents to favor the Y chromosome, throwing the skein of her fingers at them, in and out, up and down, witchily, then she got up from the kitchen table and went to get the mail at the front door (because the mail slot's lid had clanked just at that moment), and she returned with a letter from a lawyer saying that the rich aunt had died; and while it didn't name the figure that would come to them, they knew all about it, and they knew it would be a lot. Lotta dangled the page of the letter before them and declared, "Now you can definitely afford him." So that was one day. Then a year later, they brought Audrey limping home from the hospital on an empty afternoon, having left the boy back there, a late-term abortion is so profound, and at home under the mail slot, because the year of legal formalities had ended, was the final notice of bank transfer: a sum of money had become theirs that, they'd all admitted, could lift them to an unaccustomed new life, if they wanted it. In magical terms, the sacrifice of a child had made an open place for the cash to arrive, and nobody liked the feeling of that deal. The situation was never phrased aloud, but that's how it felt. *He* wasn't here for it.

So squandering some few thousand dollars, for starters, seemed right. Five thousand wasn't much, if it would do something to lift Lotta out of the tailspin she had been falling into. When picking her up or dropping her off at school, he had seen her trailing around by herself, preferring the side entrance over the main entrance, veering, somehow haltered, while other girls swam freely in large groups and pairs. Or if she were with a group, she'd be applying herself to the outer circle, in an excluded sort of way, pessimistically. The Lotta who'd once been so independent minded had started adopting opinions and slang and mannerisms all drawn from the very circle that was excluding her. At home she spent her time in her room with the door closed, researching private schools, conversing by Internet with her cousins in Connecticut, planning her escape. He really believed that her present drama of grief, over the deleted little brother, was a cover-up for her worse dread. Teenagers' dread is their discovery of personal irremediable defects and second-rateness. In high school you present yourself to the marketplace. You hadn't been aware there was a marketplace. That's the terrible open floor. You enter through the main entrance. You're suddenly out on that floor. On schoolday mornings he would drop her off on the curb and he could see it descend upon her, at the moment of her climbing to set foot in those corridors, he could see it in the set of her shoulders: her irremediable defects and second-rateness.

So they sent in their Fantasy Vacations deposit and went ahead with it, because they all knew perfectly well, even *while* signing up, that it was going to be phony-baloney, the "Live Concert" and the "MTV-Style Video" and the "Complete Stylist's Makeover." The brochure advised: "*Sometimes in life, you can store away a memory of how wonderful you are. That's an investment. That's forever,*" and Lotta, reading it, made vomit sounds. They knew the whole experience would be a fun house ride, and beneath their dignity. Lotta had told *none* of her friends at school about it. Nobody. She kept it a secret. That seemed sad. Yet Mark found he hadn't, either, mentioned it at work.

SHE MAY HAVE alighted on a Sunset Boulevard curbstone wearing a red dress with a slit, but the only way he could picture her was as intelligent. Under the neon lights among the passersby, she would have an instinct of self-esteem, and self-preservation. She would do something smart like find a safe, brightly lit diner to take a booth in. She had her phone, and she had money. She just wanted to get out of the limo and distance herself from Bodie the Octopus. She could always call a cab.

Nevertheless, the dress did have a slit hem; and inside him the prediction of anguish was always sore and always shedding, and he pulled out his cell phone and dialed her again. This time it went straight to voice mail.

So that would mean she was talking to someone.

Which must be a good sign. It would be Bodie. She was quarreling with him. Or maybe she had called her mother at home, if she were very upset.

"Her phone's busy." He looked at Blythe, and she at him. They both knew, she was talking to Bodie. There was that lift in Blythe's brow.

He looked around. They were stuck at a stoplight. All Los Angeles continued to look like local news crime-scene footage. Here was a typical strip mall: a liquor store, a Thai noodle place, a store for automotive parts, a shop selling voodoo and Santeria equipment, and a clothing outlet called Dress Barn. Out front on the curb, a woman in a sexy miniskirt stood fondling her feather boa. But it was obviously a man, from the bony hips in the skirt and the wig's bumped-up architecture all bronzed under streetlamps. His fingertips played sensually on the rim of a large sign, hand scrawled in aerosol spray paint on a sheet of plywood: GET SMOGGED HERE.

At green, Blythe's car took off.

"People here like to drive," Mark grumbled. He'd noticed increasingly in California, and everywhere else, too, the same chain stores were starting to appear every few miles, recycling past—a Taco Bell, a Gap, a Kentucky Fried, a Blockbuster Video—then further on, a Taco Bell, a Gap, a Kentucky Fried, another Blockbuster—so the neighborhood stays roughly similar, similarly consumable everywhere, and he was reminded of the backgrounds in old movies, a continuous mural that was rolled past by stagehands. In cartoons, too, when the animated character walked, the same tree stump would keep coming around again, the same cloud again, and the same pine tree again.

"Don't make fun of Los Angeles," Blythe answered his observation about driving.

"By the way, that's awful. About Rod, your boyfriend. That's a really awful experience for *you*."

He'd thought of it because this neighborhood looked like, probably, just the kinds of streets Rod was alone on, during his last days, when he was "on the street," a goblin, befriended by people like the feather-boaed transvestite. She had mentioned, in a little additional detail, that Rod moved "in a sort of lobster way" after it got too hard to walk upright. Surely street life was hard on his hairdo. Maybe she had a chance sometimes to get him inside and clean him up. She hadn't said whether he was alone outside when he died.

"I live not far from here," she remarked, confirming his thinking exactly. "Right up that way."

She had gestured to a dark, broad side street, an industrial-looking area. Nothing was parked at the curbs, only occasional Dumpsters. Imagine calling such a desolate place your "neighborhood." He reminded himself that Blythe, like Wonder Woman in disguise, was also an art appraiser, and that she had graduated from Risdie, so her home, in that industrial area, would be one of those arty lofts with vast spaces, Persian rugs, a cappuccino machine.

He said, "I didn't mean to be insensitive, saying Rod's hair was like somebody in comic books."

His imperturbable L.A. girl at the steering wheel—tough as her own Subaru, handling the wheel with the grappling grip habitual to Subaru girls—shed all offense with a shake of her head. "He did. Look like Veronica in the *Archie*s. Everybody said so. You're not the first. He was vain of his hair."

She took her eyes off the road and looked straight across at Mark to tell him, "Rod and I were high school sweethearts." As if it explained everything.

It did explain a lot. First they were sweethearts. That was romantic. Then later, Rod, the artistic one, became *a responsibility*. And Blythe was The Responsible One.

"Did he go to college?" he asked, comparing Rod's life with Blythe's life. She had her good Risdie education.

"He went to UCLA, but only for a year. He dropped out."

So the boyfriend had the role of wild artist—the musician, the creative one. Mark was somewhat familiar with the psychology of the relationship because he himself had been so wayward in his career as a physicist. Audrey the lawyer. Him the deadbeat. But deadbeat with tenure, a contented deadbeat, deadbeat chauffeuring his daughter to piano lessons, deadbeat with a new history of brain lacunae and mental lapses, serving on departmental committees wordlessly without making any contributions, first out the door when the meeting's over, then at home putting on the apron in the evening to make his Famous Chili or his Famous Hamburgers or his Famous Mulligatawny. Tenure is a kind of gangrene not at all painful, so you don't have to be aware you've got it, but tenure definitely put a fortunate cordon sanitaire around *him* including the UC-system medical and dental and retirement and death benefits.

It was a smooth relevancy, then, when he went back to Blythe's other topic, complaining, "Yes, I used to be controversial." She would know he was referring to his apparitions on YouTube. It was an admission of his fecklessness, his kinship with guys like even the asshole Rod, and males' prized inconstancy and failure proneness. All guys are alike. Physicist. Pedal steel player. Casualties all.

She checked her mirror and changed lanes. "The Internet has plenty. People with various opinions. As if *I* understood the first thing about theoretical physics." Her hand lifted and made a rolling motion conjuring up all the mysteries of the universe as endless scarves in air to be tossed, and then she named one: "'Fossils.' Time and space are '*fossils*'?"

The slit-hem dress on Sunset Boulevard was a picture always at the back of his mind. The bare arms. The teetery high heels on a curbstone.

"That was points and instants," he said. "I was against 'the point.' And I was against 'the instant.' I wanted to enlarge the dimensionless instant. And enlarge the dimensionless point. So . . ." Through the windshield he faced the coming flow. His own old work felt like it might have been something on an exam he'd taken long ago. "So the instant in time and the point in space are fossils, in something called the 'block' view of time. Time is a block." He glanced. "We are all inside the big bang."

And he looked away. He had glanced to see if any of this was taking hold. Or mattered. During this drive Blythe's hip at his left side—pithy, elfin, erotic, blue-jeaned—was blinkered from his sight, so as to magically avert the *actual forfeiture* of a daughter. He would not *look* at this woman so long as Lotta was in danger. Los Angeles kept parting for them as her little car slipped at top speed through green light after green light. One of his superstitious ceremonies had come back to comfort him: both hands were thrust deep in his pants pockets, knees together, heels together, elbows clamped to his sides, a method for a passenger to ward off, via personal symmetry, any possibility of an accident. At the bottommost corners in his pockets, his fingers discovered the day's supply of ibuprofen, eight of the little brown pills divided evenly between his two pockets. It was how he loaded himself for any outing, indeed every morning, and he fingered the pills, symmetrically in unison, in both pocketed hands, one-two-three-four, one-two-three-four, a bracelet repeating itself in flowing over his fingers. Here in Los Angeles, all around was a city driven by ambition, every fiber of its soul afire with ambition, swarmed by newcomers, all with desires, desires for an answer from the world, desires to sing their song for the assembled many, or do their stand-up comedy routine and get laughs, or have their screenplay produced, or just *write* their screenplay, or to be beautiful, to be beloved, to get attention. Or just to have a nice house.

This was the weekend of the annual physics meeting, tonight, right now this very minute in Karlsruhe, in Germany, and he hadn't said anything about it. He wasn't in Karlsruhe; he was here instead. He hadn't mentioned anything to Lotta anyway. As for Audrey back home, he'd spoken of it only once with her, some time ago, and it was in a moment when she wasn't listening. He didn't even himself like to think of it. So why bring it up?

"Here we are," said Blythe, pulling up at a curb, to park in a dim lull between streetlights.

★ HE LOOKED AROUND—FOR something like a chain restaurant or a coffee shop, or some obvious meeting place. But there was none. They'd pulled up at the sidewalk beside a plain armored door. It bore a small, stenciled, faint old identification: STUDIO LOT, the pigment mostly bleached away by, perhaps, the sulfur dioxide of the eternal city. But there was a card taped up, which could only be the work of the Fantasy Vacations office, "Closed Tonight, for an *EXCLUSIVE* Private Party!" in the font of somebody's office computer. It wasn't even a card, it was a page of white printer paper—and the word *EXCLUSIVE* had been pinned at one corner by a starry-twinkle graphic, to bathe it in glamour, bathe it in limelight, bathe it in others' envy, envy lifeblood of the economy, universal currency in this city stretching for miles all around. Lotta was still out somewhere. The fact that her phone had been busy—and the fact that the boy Bodie had set out alone into the night from the hotel—it all added up to the likelihood that the two of them were commencing some further intrigue.

Mark was crabbing around in the Subaru's bucket seat to search up and down along this dim section of Sunset. The only thing nearby was a storefront across the street whose display window was outlined in marquee lights selling frothy pink bikinis and "toys."

He got out his phone. "I think I'll give her another try."

Blythe was standing outside the car while he still sat inside.

He told her, "We should get that boy Bodie's cell phone number."

"We'll get it from Billie," she said. She'd already thought of it.

Sitting there inside the car while she watched him, he reached Lotta's recording again, but immediately, with no rerouting click. She had turned her phone off. So she knew about his voice mail messages, and now she had turned her phone off to shut him out.

★ THERE TO GREET them at the Studio Lot, when they came in, was fifteen-year-old Danny Banzinetti standing beneath his downpour of incapacitating hair, his electric guitar slung on. The guitar went with him everywhere, slung just like that. "Heard anything?" he said. He lifted himself up from against the wall, and he actually stood forward on his own two feet, which was a lot for Danny: people here were worried.

Blythe said, "Hi, Danny. Is Billie here? Where is everybody?"

"They're all in there."

The Studio Lot was a twilight, shimmering place. At the far end of a concrete floor burnished glossy brown, there was a full bar, its backlit shrine crowded with flasks of colorful potions. Mark traveled in Blythe's wake while she explained the place. "It's a juice bar on our nights here. On our nights, they close to the public and put away the real liquor. So it's for youngsters, but it's made up to be as evil-looking as grown-up places."

She added, "Gee, I guess they sent the camera home." It was a measure of how Lotta's disappearance had changed the evening: the turtlenecked paparazzo wasn't in evidence loitering with his big old-fashioned flashbulb reflector, probably always glad to be let off duty.

Sitting around a little table were five Celebrities, the five who tonight hadn't bolted from the fold: the lovebirds Rachel and Josh; David, the gay one from Chicago; Chang the Elvis impersonator from Vancouver, who was so shy offstage he never spoke; and Danny Banzinetti the fifteen-year-old glam-rock guitar hero in tight leather pants. Danny had been the closing act tonight, wincing, twitching, his finger delving in his guitar's most sensitive sore spot high up, making it scream. The only other customers in the bar were the kids' limo drivers. There were two of them—recognizable by the fancy chauffeurs' livery they were obliged to wear as part of this particular gig—sitting on tall stools at the bar nursing their vitamin waters or smoothies. There was no chair for Mark, so the Muslim from La Jolla, Josh, sprang up smoothly and took a chair from the next table.

Blythe said, "Where are the chaperones?" as she sat down among the Celebrities.

"Getting a drink. They wanted a real drink," said the Muslim's girlfriend Rachel, with a nod indicating somewhere up the street. "But our drivers can babysit us."

These were a group of teenagers who could surely "babysit" themselves—David the gay one was a polite, top-of-his-class student; Chang, when offstage, took the world so seriously he had a tic of blinking and swallowing hard; and Josh was such a devout Muslim convert, he exemplified what Lotta's generation was calling a Straight-Edge (he'd made a disapproving frown at the mention of the chaperones' weakness for a "real drink")—they all had such obvious integrity on display, and all radiated such a brightness of unopposed hope and belief and aspiration, an old grown-up like Mark knows to stay far clear from so pure a radiance, and not risk quenching it. Maybe only Danny Banzinetti could have any pretenses to corruption; but they would be pretenses only; he happened to be from Mark's part of the world, Marin County, and Mark had a familiar picture of the kind of genial incontinent Marin will breed, innocent, artless, guilt-free scoundrels. He had watched such boys this year taking absolutely no interest in his daughter, as if she were invisible to them, or as if she passed along in a separate, alternate dimension of space-time. As a lazy father, he was slightly grateful for that state of affairs in its holding pattern.

"You know . . ." he spoke up at the table in his paternal voice.

The young Celebrities had been excluding him, from their vision and from their circle of communion naturally, because he's The Father; and it's an axiom: when fathers enter the scene, the fun is over, all fairy-tale problems are going to be squarely addressed, all drama and make-believe will have fallen rumpled to the floor. Instinctively kids will sense a grown man's more sagacious hopelessness, disguise it how he may.

"You're all being very solicitous, but Carlotta is smart, and I'm not worried about her. I understand she's upset. But she's smart." This he said. But it was in contradiction to the steady, visceral pinching. The pinching was there. It wouldn't stop until he found her. She was out on Sunset Boulevard in her red chanteuse dress. But then as he looked at the five faces around the table, he had a funny realization: he realized that they weren't genuinely worried about her. There was no true anxiety here. He realized they saw Lotta's adventure tonight from some better-informed perspective.

"Lotta has a guru," explained Rachel dryly.

She looked at David then.

And everybody looked at David. David was the spokesman, the arbiter of the group, the articulate one, the Ivy League–bound one. He tilted his head to one side, in a sort of elaborate apology for the news he was about to impart, and his long, beautiful hands made shrugging motions, explaining all this to the new-arrived Mr. Perdue. "She has started subscribing to Bodie's . . . *influence*. Bodie is . . . *complicated*."

Danny Banzinetti confided, "This is Bodie's second year here"— darkly, as if that were evidence of a louche sophistication. Having said it and drawn attention to himself, Danny looked pained. He readjusted his guitar and jerked his hair. It was awkward for Danny with that guitar strapped on at all times. Especially whenever it came time among people to sit down, he had to keep adjusting it as the neck thrust up from below and needed to be squashed and suppressed or thrust aside. The boy's hair, too, menaced him. It was hard being Danny Banzinetti just at this age.

"One *aspect* of Bodie," said David, while his octave-span hands began the spectacle of pouring out this *aspect* of Bodie before them all, and then kneading it up, stroking it taller, into a little lumpy icon of a personality, "is that he has had to adapt, you know, *adapt* to life, as a quote disabled person unquote. And *grow* into that. Bodie has all the natural desires, and drives, and wishes. But he will always be limited, physically. That must be a very difficult thing to face at a young age. To face the wrongness of it."

So spoke David. At *his* young age. Whenever Mark encountered the other Celebrities—in a studio control booth, or at the soundstage rehearsals, or just waiting in the hotel lobby for the cars to come around—he got to see what Blythe claimed she loved in this job: they were always a peculiar group of young people who got off the planes at LAX, every two weeks a new small crop. But at the moment he was sitting here talking about *his own* Celebrity daughter, who had gone missing, and the stomach knot, which he was not focusing on, consisted in the fact that his own girl was somewhat ostracized—perhaps self-ostracized, but nevertheless—because everybody at this table had a distinct visual image of some specific sexual charity she had performed in the back seat of a car. Mark's own mind, there, was an unvisitable dark well, knowing as he did her characteristic daughterly diligence.

David—who was facing, if not "disabilities," certain social injustices of his own, in the form of homosexuality amid a society that honestly would never altogether tolerate it—continued in his analysis of Bodie's personality. Which he described as "Napoleonic." He also used the adjective *compensatory*. Mark knew something of David's neighborhood, too. Because he himself had grown up in the Chicago suburbs near David's. David was born in Skokie, and then his family had moved to Winnetka. So Mark had a picture of the kind of solid house, the Midwestern seriousness, the vast safety, yet the anxiety too, the general Midwesternness that never lifts, anxiety largely over social visibility and prosperity and ambitions for the children, but it was still a liberal place back there, and David would do very well indeed. One doesn't worry about the Davids. As he went on, he was portraying Bodie Lostig as a boy who was "*really highly intelligent*" (somehow a euphemistic expression, here), a boy who was even powerful and effective in the world, but who had learned to extract his rewards from the world by exerting an intellectual dominance. To be a companion to Bodie required agreeing with his ideas. Bodie was "a philosopher," he said. And you had to "go along on his little philosophical trip."

The guru comment, back there, was slightly troubling. Mark tried to recall the songs Bodie had sung during the weekend in rehearsals. Bodie's *philosophy*, from the bits he could recall, was that you have to live every minute of your life with passion and commitment. Savor every experience, et cetera. Be all you can be. Every moment is golden.

Mark said, "As in the songs he writes?"

"Well, ah, yes, exactly," said David, his eyes tender with an ambitious young artist's standard forgiveness of mediocrity in a fellow artist.

Rachel beside him added, in her hair-curtained gloom, "Yep, that Bodie. He's intense." Her head was dropped forward so her smothered voice spoke straight into her collarbone.

Intense? They were making a two-wheeled singer of bland pop songs into a Svengali requiring submission and adulation. It would be unlike Lotta to humor a bully. To all pretension, his daughter gave instant, dispelling poof-and-shrug.

"He's holy," said Danny Banzinetti. "He won't even eat honey. And everything has to be raw. He won't eat anything cooked above a temperature of . . . ?" he looked around the circle.

"Fifty degrees centigrade," said Blythe, as a Fantasy Vacations staffer providing the information levelly without mockery or sarcasm, over the rim of her glass of wine. Somehow she had coaxed a glass of wine out of the bartender for herself.

"Yeah, and he turns the lights *off!*"

"*In the Future Perfect Society*," Danny Banzinetti used a reverberant fascist baritone, "*Nobody Will Ever Leave Their Property.*"

It seemed to be a slogan. Something to do with Bodie's philosophy.

Bodie Lostig was starting to seem not like a threat but rather more like a big bore, an oddball bore.

"Yeahmp," said Rachel, still mumbling into her collarbone. "That Bodie."

"Does anybody, by the way," said Blythe, "know Bodie's cell phone number?"

No. Nobody did. But approving looks were passed around the table: calling Bodie was a good idea. *They* should have thought of it. If anybody'd had his number.

The door to the street swung open. A businesslike woman who had to be Billie came in while poking and weeding deep in her open purse. She seemed to know who Mark was without lifting her glance from inside her purse as she addressed him, speaking down into its open jaws, "Mr. Perdue, hi, let's talk over here at the bar. I'm Billie Ahrsatz."

BILLIE AHRSATZ WAS making a place for herself on a stool at a smaller bar nearer the door, a bar dark and shut-down. At her arrival, Blythe's manner of rising to her feet made the power relationships clear: Blythe was a part-timer closer to the bottom of the Fantasy Vacations hierarchy. Also, Blythe had distanced herself rather quickly from her glass of wine. She'd probably had to exert her wiles to get it, but when Ms. Ahrsatz's back was turned she downed it and left the wet glass behind, and she and Mark went over to take tall stools with Billie at the smaller bar. This all felt as if the two of *them* were now facing justice. He reminded himself, whatever he and Blythe had desired that night, or even thought of desiring, it was none of Billie Ahrsatz's business. They hadn't even done anything. That was a saving fact, to be borne in mind. Mark had a wife at home. And Blythe had the ghost of the boyfriend Rod to answer to. They were adults, and all their personal moral choices were free of Billie Ahrsatz's censure.

She continued not looking up at them—or at anything in the bar or anywhere—taking the whole world for granted as those in authority do, while she sought in her purse for a ballpoint pen and a small pad, testing the pen on the pad to make sure it worked.

There was no bartender here at this side-bar and the overhead lights were off, so the conference felt clandestine. If the saloon could support two full bars, plainly there were nights when the Studio Lot was packed, nights when it wasn't leased out to a handful of children and stocked only with fruit juices and energy drinks. Mark began by proposing, "It would be nice if we can go on *not* involving the police. If we can find Lotta soon enough on our own . . ." He shrugged.

"*And* find Bodie," Billie corrected him, and she lifted her dark, big-as-chestnuts eyes, to focus all her attention at last on Mark.

Slight asymmetry to that face. One eye was mounted a little differently than the other. Brown hair. Coiffed in the manner of the one called Moe among the Three Stooges, the bossy one. Her suit coat had padded shoulders, so she was as big and powerful as a jumbo box of cereal.

"Yes, by all means, Bodie too," Mark agreed. "Blythe said you'd have his phone number."

"Yes, but first of all, I gather this means nobody has notified the police," she said, while again reaching for her purse, this time stirring for a cell phone.

Mark said, "No police yet. As father, I want to decree that."

Billie Ahrsatz glanced up—at Mark and his "decree"—then she dug out her phone and opened it.

He persisted, "I'm sure Lotta will get in touch. She's just embarrassed. She's just been . . . *bamboozled* by a boy with a lot of passive-type manipulation involving a made-up 'terminal illness.'"

Maybe right now he wasn't so even-tempered as he thought. Billie Ahrsatz pressed her cell phone to her heart and looked at Mark steadily. "Bodie's condition isn't made-up. Bodie's condition is congenital."

She added a baleful emphasis to that word *congenital*, a word she was applying with the wrong relevance, a word she'd plagiarized unfairly from Mark's own recent personal life. In Mark Perdue's house this spring, the word *congenital* meant something, something relevant.

74

She clarified, "*And* degenerative."

He scoffed, "Have you seen him?" It sounded callous, but all he meant was, Bodie Lostig looked more robust than anybody on the tour, with his powerful upper body, in his truncation a satyr but chaste, with his golden hair, with the cleft in his chin like the base of an apple, with his manner of punishing a drum set, and in restaurants or parking lots or recording studios his way of swinging himself crablike on his arms, from car seat to wheelchair, from wheelchair to drum throne, with the grace of a gymnast on parallel bars or side horse. He was a vital young man with a genuine bloom in his complexion, and he was a sex object to his daughter, a consideration that made Mark's heart, like an old man's, resist saying farewell to the world as it spun out of control. His own lymebrain was always suspect. Maybe it was, admittedly, time to call the police. *Not* calling the police was like the trick of healing an illness by pretending to ignore it. Such magic can work, but only up to a point. In any case Billie Ahrsatz was hitting numbers on her phone, having more authority than a father's decree, and she put the phone to her ear. She'd only hit three numbers, so it must be the 9-1-1 emergency line. "We're going to have to phone the Lostigs, too. Mr. and Mrs. In Cleveland it must be who-knows-what. Ugh. What time zone is that?"

The problem had, in one billion-trillionth of a second, expanded from toy-sized to galaxy-sized. The Lostigs of Shaker Heights were presently sleeping, no doubt heavily, in a large bedroom in their dark, peaceful time zone. Now they would have to get up, and maybe even go to the Cleveland airport—and something told Mark they wouldn't get along, he and the Lostigs. Everything he knew about parenthood, and about the Midwest of his own youth, informed him that the Lostigs would think *his* child was some sort of bad influence. He pictured Mr. Lostig as a, say, car dealer in a Ban-Lon shirt, with a powerful, heavy wristwatch and a good thin leather jacket, getting off the plane with his wife.

Also, the police would descend now. Billie had her cell phone at her ear and was averting her eyes from Mark. "No," she told the phone, "this is not an emergency. We have a situation with a young lady who's gone missing."

Mark cast an irritated-but-also-guilty look at Blythe. The expression deep in Blythe's eyes, aimed at him, meant that he needed only be patient with this woman Billie—and they would share their impressions of her later.

He sometimes really *could* have married Blythe Cress, here where things don't matter so much. It was her wise, passive eternal laxity, it made her utterly absorbent, utterly languid, so anything was all right, nothing evaluated. All that languor of hers this weekend was draped before him for the taking. Nevertheless, he was still—he was always— "Mark Perdue," and he had meanwhile taken out his own phone and hit speed dial, thinking he might give Lotta another try.

Billie was talking into her own unit, telling the 9-1-1 people, "We were hoping you could give us a number we *can* call."

As for Lotta, her reception was still turned off. (*Hi everybody, it's Carlotta . . .*) So he put it away. Billie was handing her own phone directly to him. "Here," she said. "They're transferring this to the police number. You'd better do the talking, because you're the one who will have the information they'll need. You're 'the father,'" she told him with an emphatic look.

Well, the phone was ringing, and the universe was expanding. Every instant a fossil. Billie Ahrsatz was enacting the part of a professional who took seriously her legal responsibility for seven teenagers.

And she now turned her attention, her entire box-of-cereal, around toward her employee Blythe, who as the assigned "escort" was possibly suspected of being at fault for some of this trouble.

"Los Angeles Police Department."

The man's voice, at Mark's ear, was thoroughly weary of the world outside his office. Outside L.A. police headquarters tonight it was Saturday night, the night ruled by foolish mistakes.

"Hi. My name is Mark Perdue. I'm a visitor to Los Angeles," he began, as if being a tourist would somehow privilege him. "I'm here with my daughter, and she's gone missing . . ." Saying it made his heart pound, for the first time now.

"Just a minute, I'll transfer you." He was put on hold.

And with a clotting sound in the earpiece, the intelligible universe everywhere was smothered and he was plunged into an insulted solitude. Worse than solitude, he was plunged, all unprepared, into the paucity of his life. Lotta was the main thing he had. He wasn't at the annual physics conference in Germany right now. He was here in a fashionable young L.A. bar. This weekend in Karlsruhe, everybody would be there, everybody from New York to Cambridge and Edinburgh, from Berkeley to CERN. Now Lotta had gone missing. Again, every moment a fossil.

He was letting his eyes rest on a wall of snapshots while he waited. On a bulletin board behind the bar, at least a hundred photographs were pinned up crowding and overlapping. For years the regular customers in this place had been captured by flashbulb, in their mirth, in their drunkenness, hugging and mugging and showing off, brandishing their beer bottles or their martini glasses, girls' friskiness, guys' throats exposed raw in the flash, eyes crazed. All his life he'd seen these bulletin boards in neighborhood bars, and they all blended into a single limbo, a sort of afterlife, some photos more faded than others, their chemical colors gone powdery, eclipsed by brighter, newer, overlapping photos. For the customers they perhaps stood as evidence that maybe they weren't as beautiful, that night, as they'd felt in the moment. But beauty was never the point. Everybody always knew that. Everybody was pretending beauty was the whole point. It was visible now: the shine in those people's eyes wasn't exaltation. It was fear, or deeper, panic, there in the pinholes of the pupils. The Los Angeles of the early twenty-first century had passed like a dream all around them, a dream they'd invested in. Now they were immortalized, trapped behind that gloss. Even at the flashbulb's pop, even then, they'd foreseen this afterlife. That's what every flashbulb pop is all about. And Mark, him too, he was no better, he was no different. *Avoiding* appearing in a gallery of barroom snapshots isn't going to specially enlighten anybody, or privilege anybody. All the excitement in Karlsruhe this week would be about the Large Hadron Collider. It was a time to start formally bidding to put a team on the Collider. A certain politicking would be happening all around Karlsruhe in the big modern hotel or in the old *gasthof* with the clever pastries under a glass dome, people like Seul Aspect standing genially around the dessert cart, and people like Parme Nides and Allen Aiken, all would be jockeying for time on the new machine in Geneva, where temperatures like a trillionth of a second after the big bang would soon be raging within the big magnets, generating a foam of microscopic black holes (which supposedly, according to the popular hysteria, would swell up and eat Switzerland, eat the planet, eat the solar system). Heidi Martingger was another one who wouldn't be there. Heidi was the other pariah, along with Mark, who had gone to cosmology. *He* wasn't there ostensibly because he was here in Los Angeles with the young Celebrities.

When he and Audrey had looked at the calendar and realized there was this scheduling conflict—(all on the same weekend, Karlsruhe, the Celebrity Vacation, and the Oakland "Habitat" Build-a-Thon)—Mark had *volunteered* to make the sacrifice. He'd offered. He'd be willing to skip Karlsruhe. At the moment of making that offer, he happened to be at the stove stirring his Famous Mulligatawny with a wooden spoon, winding it up to elevate its broth to a shining golden velvet. Audrey, at the kitchen table, was frowning over the calendar, seeing the conflict of dates, and he himself volunteered, "I could skip Karlsruhe this year." It felt like free-falling, while standing on his own kitchen floor, watching his mulligatawny revolve. Audrey apparently hadn't heard. She didn't answer. He looked at her and waited, but her soul was absent from the room and had been absent for a long time.

Then the cell phone at his ear was answered, "Missing Persons."

So Mark launched into this. His heart sped up. Talking to cops aroused a dread he should have been feeling all along. He was a fool. He was an idiot. "Just a minute," spoke the Asian-sounding voice, interrupting him, a young man, Vietnamese or Cambodian would have been Mark's guess. The clicking of a computer keyboard could be heard.

He began by asking for a name: not Lotta's name but *his*.

Mark didn't want to waste time on the many pages of this bureaucrat's computer form. "Wouldn't it be good to start with her? And a description? And then right away you can put out an 'APB.'"

APB was an expression he had been hearing on television police dramas since he was a child, but something in the acoustics of the phone, on the other end, made it ridiculous.

The officer said, "What's APB?"

"'All points bulletin.' All the patrol cars can begin searching for her. With her description."

"We don't do that, sir."

"You don't do that?"

"We don't look for anybody." This was something the man had said to many people before, many distraught and unreasonable people.

"What do you do, then?"

"We take your report."

"Then what do you . . . *do?*"

After a pause he said, "We don't do nothing, sir."

It was possible to start getting the picture. A big city police department lacks the manpower or resources to put out great dragnets whenever a child, somewhere in L.A., doesn't come home. Instead they have her on file. When, or if, something terrible happens, her name pops up as "reported missing."

"So *after*. Oh. Hm. I see. *After* a crime has been committed," Mark said with an immediate access to a rancor that he wasn't entitled to, and which he had had no inkling of. "*Then* you look at your information. Then you've got something so you can blame *her*. Make *her* seem like it's *her* fault, or *her* problem, whatever it is."

Before saying one more regrettable thing, he closed up the phone and set it down on the bar. He stood up off his stool, just to walk around and stretch, and go outside, get a breath of fresh air.

Billie had turned on her stool to look down at the closed-up phone on the bar, then she looked at Mark. She said, "Well, I'll have to call them."

He was headed toward the door. Involving the police felt like bad luck, that's all. For the first time, now, he pictured himself calling Audrey back home and beginning the conversation, *Sweetheart? Something has happened.*

"Fantasy Vacations has to report it," Billie reemphasized for him, as he left.

He thought he might get a breath of fresh air. See if Lotta just might happen to be right outside, right this minute coming up the street. Or at least he could have a look, out there, at the profound city she had vanished into.

T WAS AT that point—just as he'd come outside, into the city's ancient cool kiss of anonymity—that his phone was destined to ring, announcing Lotta, her distinctive ringtone, the ringtone her mom liked to refer to as "the wrongtone," a musical phrase from a pop song that, in turn, was derived from the obnoxious old melody of the schoolyard taunt. At the sound of that nagging in his coat pocket, relief and anger and thankfulness surged in him. It was amazing how empty is all the rest of life when there's love. It amounted to an unmanly dependency, on the vagaries of a girl, a subjugation of his kingship, but when this particular girlhood was over (which it already was), it would be all mulligatawny for him, from then on, in a semidetached on a cul-de-sac, and the tedious personal chess match with imaginary heart-attack sensations, TV clicker in hand.

"Hi, Dad, how's everything?" said Lotta's voice.

She was with somebody all right. Because she never said any such thing. Never, not in all her sixteen years, did she ever say *How's everything*.

"Where are you?"

"We're by the Hollywood sign. We're okay."

"'We'?"

"We're just out on an excursion."

"Excursion. Do you know what time it's getting to be?"

Of course she had met up with the boy again somehow, for some reason. But Mark wasn't going to make her go into the details. Being interrogated by your telephoning parent is always an indignity, and surely tonight her whole fragile personality would be shivering in oscillations back and forth between "starlet" and "back seat girl"; *his* only proper role was to get her on the plane tomorrow after the closing party, and get her back home, home where she could go back to being simply Lotta, "Lotta" at home, a broad wave function that *hadn't* collapsed to a specific time and place: damp bath towels and footies and scrunchies, her pajamas-plus-parka costumes, eating cheese-flavored crackers and casting her usual gloom, unwashed dishes beside the computer, televisions and radios playing in empty rooms.

She said, "I thought I'd call because I saw all these times you called tonight when I checked my messages."

"Excursions are great, Lotta, but it's going to be midnight, and this is an unfamiliar city, and you've got a recording session tomorrow."

"It's not a recording session, it's a video shoot, *supposedly*."

"Where are you?" he said, adding, "Which, in any case, you want to be rested for. And get a good night's sleep."

She didn't answer, and Mark just waited, because that—right there—was the form an ultimatum took. At least with him. She would know now. It was inevitable. Wherever she was, he would come get her. In Blythe's Subaru.

He just didn't want to have to face Bodie, his weird personal beauty, his self-certainty. The Winnetka boy David, in dissecting Bodie's personality, had talked of *compensatory strategies*, one of which was *heroism*, and the word summed up everything that was invincible about "Bodie." On the phone he listened for background sounds, but the circuit was silenced by the low-pass filters they use, erasing everything below a few kHz. Quiet as velvet. She must be outside in the night air somewhere, and he imagined her standing under one of those palms that clatters in the L.A. breeze, her boyfriend beside her in his wheelchair.

"We've got Blythe's car," he said, which was his way of asserting that they would come get her right away. "Be a bit of a comedown from the fancy limos. You'd be slumming, with us. By the way, darling, you were great tonight. Onstage I mean. People were standing up out of their seats." He'd already told her all this, backstage. "Literally, people stood up. You were electrifying."

Such praise was a way of *tightening* the screws on Lotta. This according to the logic of a secret esoteric code of fatherhood. Or at least his fatherhood. And her daughterhood.

She sighed under the pressure and whined, "Oh Dad . . ."

So he actually felt remorse, administering one more small humiliation tonight.

"Dad? We really don't need to do the so-called video shoot tomorrow. I'm not going to. Neither of us are."

He'd underestimated this.

Ordinarily she might have bounced right back. She had an even ruthless ability, ordinarily, to forget about any chagrin within five minutes.

"Well, Lotta, why not?"

Stupid question. Wrong angle.

"Do you want to go home?"

She said, "No, no, not at all. It's expensive changing the tickets. Let's just stick with the reservations we have now."

"But you might regret not having something to look at later, Lott. Posterity! And who knows . . . ? When you're famous . . . ?"

"No, Dad, I've been doing some thinking. Doing a lot of thinking. This isn't the moment, right now, but sometime I'd be happy to discuss my thinking with you."

That was clearly a remark she had delivered while looking into the eyes of Bodie there with her. She'd never in her life spoken in such a way, with a social worker's calm condescension.

"Let's discuss your thinking right now. If it might involve changing our plane tickets."

She said right away, "I'm reordering my priorities, and I'm going to be a humbler person, starting now. Or I'm going to try."

This was Bodie. Bodie was helping her reorder her priorities. Helping her become a humbler person.

It wasn't necessary for him to pry, because she went right on, airing her new thinking, "I actually think most people are incredibly selfish. Selfishness is the whole thing. The sooner *anybody* can be a larger human being, the better."

He had to wait a minute, and allow the beguiling new rhetoric to die away ringing.

Then he started out, "Lotta, music isn't selfish, music is a gift."

Oh, but now there was fatigue in his voice, because he *was*, face it, tired.

And she and Bodie did have plenty of taxi money, and he remembered she'd gone out wearing her sneakers instead of high heels. And he was starting to get a handle on this situation, and it was all feeling like a dreamily predictable fiasco, all too tiring to stand here and take apart. It was still long before midnight. His daughter was only going through a new phase—maybe it was a kind of moralistic trend. Which was a relief. Considering the alternatives.

"Dad?" she read his mind, "You can go to bed. We're totally fine. I'm with Bo, and we'll take a cab home eventually. We've got plenty of money. We're not in a dangerous neighborhood. This is Hollywood! Nothing's going to happen! It's Hollywood!"

"Why don't you just tell us where you are, and we'll come get you."

She put the phone to her chest for a sec to muffle it.

With his ear against the nap of silence, he remembered she had a sweater, a yellow cardigan, to cover up the red dress she'd performed in. She'd put it on backstage. So she was wearing the sweater *and* the canvas high-top sneakers.

When her voice returned, she said, "Really, Dad, I'm hanging up. Now don't worry your head about anything. Go back and get a good night's sleep. I'm having a wonderful time this whole weekend. Really. I'm grateful for all this. Good night, now. I'll see you tomorrow. If not before. 'Cause we won't be long. We won't stay out late. Love you."

She hung up. He knew her phone would go straight back to *off* and he'd been shut out again.

★ BLYTHE SAID AS she swung the car through a left turn, back toward the hotel, "I guess I'll just . . . drop you off?" She made it sound like a forlorn prospect. "And I guess that's the whole weekend?"

As if they might do anything else.

It was the wrong thing to say—she knew it too—and Mark fled straight to the topic of his daughter. "So she claims she is reordering her priorities," he complained.

He had been watching the streets go by. He just kept on doing that.

"She has decided that selfishness is an evil everywhere. She's not going to be selfish anymore. She's going to be humble. Does Bodie have some kind of . . . *cult* he's in?"

As they came to a cross street, a midnight L.A. Rollerblader with powerful thighs, elevated by his skates to the stature of the god Mercury, flashed through the boulevards at top speed. Maybe they're a common sight in Los Angeles, frequent as neutrinos, and just as safe. If the city is safe for a rollerblader, in his tight shorts, it would be safe for a sixteen-year-old in a red dress and a yellow cardigan, under the protection of a boy in a wheelchair.

Blythe mused, "And she didn't say where they were?"

"She said they're near a big billboard. A Hollywood sign."

"Oh!" Blythe was cheered. "*The* Hollywood Sign," she gestured out at the omnipresent monument in the American night, and it connected in his head—his doubtless naive, professorial head—above Los Angeles there's a famous row of giant letters staggering along a hillside spelling out HOLLYWOOD. "Do you know how to get there?"

Yes she did: she had poked her elbows out at angles, and she'd begun checking over her shoulder, pecking in all her mirrors, looking for a chance to hang a U.

However, on second thought, she pushed herself back down in her seat, holding the steering wheel at the length of her straight arms, she had such a darling little form. "I do know how to get there. But there's no '*there*.' You don't reach the actual sign. You get nowhere near. It's fenced off with, like . . . fencing. It's got different neighborhoods. Some properties back up to it. An open space backs up to it. But you just *view* it from different places. Like different vicinities. You never actually get there."

Mark watched her chipmunk profile, all the wisdom of Los Angeles behind that green gaze. A life he would never know. Lip he would never kiss. Apartment-loft he would never visit. She was born here—saw some of the East Coast in college—but then came back here. She had a beautiful knack for hitting every green light, like a sparrow, native of these woods, who threads the dense branches at top speed.

She said, "We could go there and drive around."

She looked over at him. We're all doomed to our own singular, unique, unrepeatable lives: he had spent his years as husband to Audrey, physicist at Berkeley, owner of a semidetached in Cobblestone Hearth Village Estates. Now his daughter was going to move in with her cousins in Connecticut, and at work, he secretly couldn't comprehend the new gauge-symmetry theories.

"Sure," he said.

Why not. Go there and drive around.

In fact, he wasn't sure.

Blythe seemed doubtful, too. She kept on going without turning. "There's nowhere to 'drive around' exactly. I would hardly know whether to go to Griffith Park? Like Los Feliz? Or up on Mulholland? The problem is, each approach you'd try, each has its own complicated, separate way of getting there. The land all around it is chopped up in slanty ways. There is no *place* called Hollywood Sign. Not on Earth. It's just a thing that can be viewed *from* places on Earth."

Mark stayed settled deep in the passenger seat. "I'll tell you frankly: I'm just not worried about her, because she really does have good judgment." When he'd remembered her black canvas high-top sneakers, it did something to restore his confidence in Lotta's toughness and her agility in situations.

But Blythe didn't exactly believe him. After a while she said, "*Wanna* go drive around?" She checked on him with a glance.

These were their last minutes together alone, they both knew it, and she wasn't making it any easier.

"No. She's got her cell phone. She said she'd be back soon. She *implied* I might even still be awake at the hotel when they come back."

All this was really about the imminent scene under the marquee of the hotel at the curbside, where they would say good night—which, because tomorrow was busy, would be their personal farewell—under the broad overhang where the light was so theatrical and the brass glinted. Rather than stopping in at the bar. Rather than coming up to his room for a nightcap. This had been their main collaboration all this weekend: to close off avenues, to baste quickly over any opening possibilities.

In that general effort, he added, "Lotta was funny. She told me to get a good night's sleep. Reverse roles, for father and child."

"Well, you'll have my number. If she calls. If you do want to go out and get her. My place is about ten minutes."

Efficiently they had put away the possibilities again.

The postmidterm lull at Berkeley would be succeeded by the little annoying crisis of finals. Soon Lotta would escape to a private school and she would begin the fall semester on the East Coast. And from there on out, there would be only the threat of Dodd. What empty nesters do is get a dog. He'd always been glad *not* to have a dog, to have to walk, to feed, to bend over and pinch up the craps of, on people's lawns. All pets had been barred from the house, by Lotta's allergies. Maybe there were breeds of dogs that didn't cause sneezing, so Lotta could still visit—little ugly-type dogs, stubby-type dogs, hairless little dogs. Instead of a daughter.

The Subaru swung around a left turn, and then another sudden left, and there was the hotel, his L.A. hotel, *not* the big plain Novotel in Karlsruhe on Festplatz with the row of fountains out front, where right now the world's physicists were separating out into affinity groups. "Mark Perdue" was absent from that scene. "Mark Perdue" might not even be mentioned. All the people from his department who were now in Germany, they all *wanted* to be there. Mark had years ago lost interest in the experimental side because the "facts" it produces are so fictitious and so promiscuous, too often merely artifacts of an experimental design. Supposing a critical-mass "black hole" really does get generated accidentally in the new Collider in Switzerland, it would begin by swallowing the pretty little suburban villages of

Geneva—Saint-Genis-Something—with its garden café—just at the season when the fields all around would be coming up green. Calculations were, it wouldn't suck in the entire solar system. According to calculations, the baby black hole would be born pinhole-sized among the huge Swiss magnets, and within a nanosecond it would swallow the sun and the inner planets, but wouldn't get the outer planets. Before the hole grew monstrous enough, there would be one instant, theoretically, when the gas giants Jupiter and Saturn and Uranus and Neptune could be flung out into space, fleeing the new empty center eternally, yo-yos released from their strings.

At the hotel entrance Blythe pulled the car up too short, in the dim margin of curbside space outside the blaze of lightbulbs. She put it in park and she cut the engine, and with a sigh, she turned and threw herself back against the driver's-side door, freed one thigh from under the steering wheel, cocked her knee against the gearshift console, and she said, "Rod—" shaking her head, rolling her eyes, "he used to snarf water up in his nostrils all the time."

—Which had nothing to do with anything.

—Or it was supposed to lead somewhere. Mark mirrored her, leaning back against his own door, pulling an ankle up, grateful for this.

They looked into each other's eyes. They both knew there would be no nightcap. Maybe they were both smiling a little over that shared knowledge. She would see him to the hotel door, but then there would be only a good-bye under the marquee, separated by a gap, standing each on his separate tectonic plate.

For a minute he actually hadn't quite placed the *Rod* reference. That might be Lyme disease disorientation. If it *were* a bit of lyme-brain, it didn't throw him off. He said, "A lot of people do that. Nasal irrigation. Healthy for the sinuses. They sell special solutions. And a little squirty bulb."

But she was undergoing a transformation. A tired expression had been coming up in her face, and now he scarcely recognized his Blythe there, she looked so haggard. She was coming out of a decade-long tunnel, the tunnel of Rod's prolonged death scene, crawling on the sidewalks, the opera of it. She answered with only a straying of the head, which meant: no, in Rod's case, it was no such dainty health regimen. Probably nasal irrigation would have had something to do with a cocaine habit. The damage it does to the nasal septum.

She had slipped into staring off to one side, into history. Mark kept his mild smile on her, and then he closed his eyes—signifying that he was fine, she could say more if she wanted. Plainly this discussion was the reason for stopping here and turning off the engine. On the topic of Rod she would have lots to unburden herself of. There would be regrets, old anguish piling up, things that can't be discussed with friends and family. Friends and family are too close for complaints or confessions, whereas he, for this weekend, was transient enough and alien enough to seem a perfect confessor.

In fact, however, watching Los Angeles textile appraiser Blythe Cress's concise, vulnerable body across from him—the pulse point at her throat, her skin all over salty with incipient freckles—Mark Perdue was aware he was no mild priest-confessor: her jacket lay open, and her thin sweater fabric was hammocked between the promontories of nipples and a drifted hip. A necessary base of male desire is that it's fundamentally impolite, it's fundamentally a very rude, very bad idea. What it wants to do to a female is to literally get on top and reduce her to mindlessness, maybe that's not the deliberate intention, but it's what happens in the end, and you have to want to undertake to do this to somebody with her own dignity and sensibilities and rights. It didn't feel the least bit amazing that, as a husband and father, far from home in a Los Angeles hotel, he could want to kindle the wonderful little cheap bonfire, the same old bonfire any two people can kindle; it was plain she would allow it, if he started something, she would comply, and if he proposed yet further adventures, she would comply. All that was in her languor, decked out for him. And if this were the end of it, too, she would comply; because she was compliant. That's why a life with her would be so erotic, and so endless. Sitting here toying with the Mr. Hyde personality in himself, it was probably time to pop the door and get his body out into the chill of the Los Angeles air. Go upstairs and wait up, awake, for his daughter to come home from her outing. If the days of kindling that easy bonfire were in his past now—and if it was true his daughter was such an independent operator now—and if he indeed considered it as irrelevant whether the Swiss supercollider could scare up a Higgs boson—then what was there for him, from here on out, but his Famous Mulligatawny? The apron and ladle. And twenty more years of intro courses in the 401 lecture hall. Once, this spring, he'd had a kind of sad nightmare. He'd dreamed he stood at the little podium, and in the dream, his lecture notes for the intro courses had become so smudgy over the years with erasures and interpolations, and the notebook paper had grown so tender in disintegration, he had actually had his lecture notes permanently laminated, between panes of heavy clear plastic, like five-mil acrylic, so they were outsize *cards*, as stiff as Denny's menus in a little stack on his lectern, indestructible, so that he might spill on them, or drop them on the floor, or drool on them, or whatever, and they'd be easy to clean up, good as new. They could even, after his own retirement, be passed on to another professor. And in the nightmare, that too was one more clever little economy.

Blythe said, "It wasn't just morning and evening. It got where it was every twenty minutes. Every twenty minutes, get up and stick his whole face in the basin, and snarf like a water buffalo."

She then said, "We were both waiting for him to die," and she brought her eyes to his. "And kind of working on it. On that. That probably isn't unusual for people. But this was years. This was for years. He knew it, too. He knew it was his job. It was an agreement. It just *took* forever. And then you realize you always did have this agreement, even back when you were innocent, that agreement was there. Or *thought* you were innocent. Can you imagine that? The whole . . ." she lifted her arms in an embrace, to create fanfare around this whole scene he was to imagine.

So Mark backed up and tried, then, to picture such a situation. She must mean, essentially, that Rod had been a kind of guy who dramatized himself and that "death" was always the promised ending of his drama. A dark romanticism. *Before* the HIV infection. Well, if the man had always been using Blythe as a player in his personal opera, it would have involved a terrible form of vanity on his part. Maybe it was a kind of love of disappointment. That's all Mark could imagine. This man Rod should have had a lot to live for. He had prosperity in his record store, and he had his own musical talent, whanging away on the pedal steel guitar. And of course Blythe, most of all, he had *her*, a woman he apparently squandered somehow—mistook somehow—unable to quite see the actual woman outside the blur of his own gestures.

"Was it used records?"

She stared into the bright applause of the hotel marquee, then nodded her head. "Exclusively. Used."

She believed *she'd* failed. Failed in love or attentiveness.

"This 'agreement' you apparently had . . . ?"

"Oh, years, way early, we were totally collaborating."

She saw these collaborations of theirs as evil, from the beginning collaborating in euthanasia. She tugged the halves of her jacket together. A little twitch of a smile: she was thankful, while also she was ashamed, or at least embarrassed, to be recruiting him suddenly to hear all this, at the end of the visit, their last time together. The Celebrity Vacation would end tomorrow afternoon when she would take him and Lotta to the airport on their last ride. They would never see each other again like this. So, in any intimacy, an efficiency would be necessary. There seemed in her some urgency moreover to leave a particular mysterious stain here.

Mark said, "He was a talented musician. He had a lot to live for."

She'd been staring away into the light. "He didn't *like* anything," she said, turning back again, catching his gaze. "He loved himself, I guess you could say. But not really. He *didn't* love himself. He was selfish, yes, definitely, he was basically dominated by that. He was a total schemer that way. But he hated himself. He was a monster. Everybody loved *him*."

"Everybody loved *him* . . ." Mark was leading her on.

"Oh, he was a shining star. He was wonderful."

"You knew him since high school."

She didn't answer.

With sidelong eye, she was looking back.

He said, "Hard on *you*, though. The appointed executioner."

She seemed a little startled, or even threatened, by his having jumped so far forward, so fast. They had plunged steeply into an oversimplification, sucking in everything, all of her Southern California, too steep and too fast. But then she granted him the point, tentatively, standing at the rim of the oversimplification, "Ah so," with possibly a little amusement, possibly a little gratitude. (She, after all, was the one who'd gone in and used the word *monster*.)

"Hard for you. Easy for him," he said.

Then right away, he corrected himself.

"That is, of course, dying is hard work for him or for anybody, to go through the dying thing, even *with* all the anesthetic he might have had. But you had the moral hard part, and still have it, if you were the one who was supposed to help it happen."

She was trying to take a new view of her story as it was being, here, trimmed into a certain shape. But maybe it was exactly the shape she herself wanted.

At last she said, "Little by little," grimly.

She meant *Little by little killing him*; but that wasn't Mark's invention, not really; she was the one who'd implied it, the enabler described in addiction literature, from the very beginning standing to one side, holding the vial. No doubt it *was* hard. A human body is a hard thing to kill in the end. Even if it's in poor health, the body is such a well-built, well-evolved vital organism, built to withstand batterings and expel poisons. That was the only way to picture the man's and the woman's existence together in their arty loft with a pedal steel guitar standing in the corner. The body, in its survival throes, does turn into a monster, and so the homicidal nurse, too, is transformed, inhuman in the mirror image of her victim, so Blythe didn't recognize herself, as she wrestled. It would have required a transcendent effort, even in this case, even with the steady collaboration of the victim. And Blythe, she'd been young. Young to be involved in all that. They'd started as high school sweethearts.

He went on, "Rod could help hasten the process, but . . . Those are the rules, I guess."

"Mm . . . Those were the rules."

There is no silence like the silence of a parked car.

She was certainly being frank, about a strange and disturbing part of her life. It was almost unrealistic, this whole conversation. In some sense it was possible that this conversation "wasn't really happening." In the sense that it would be filed under *irrelevant*. Or filed under *preposterous*. Or filed under *nonactionable*. Mark's whole personal future lay ahead of him. And you only keep what's relevant.

Far down the street, a figure in a hooded sweatshirt jaywalked across the empty boulevard, carrying an old paper shopping bag. If one judges people by their shoes, then he didn't seem homeless or poor. They looked like bright new athletic shoes. He crossed the street and, while Mark watched, the man dwindled along the sidewalk, at last to be swallowed where the streetlamp light failed. One more apparition who is, to all appearances, alive. And alive in his own reckoning, too. Like everybody. And carrying a personal "history." Which accounts for his evident "personality." His gait, crossing the street, implied you couldn't call him crazy and, so, "depersonalize" him. He walked like one who was whatever normal is. What's in the shopping bag. Possibly gym clothes. Possibly ingredients for a meal. His favorite thing: Hamburger Helper. Probably he's headed for the place he calls home.

Mark added, "If, as you say, this Rod was personally, psychologically, *built* so that there was no way out for him."

I.e., maybe Rod was a man who'd had only lovelessness, as his sole resource, his ace card. Deep at the bottom of his personal bag of tricks, his survival kit, was lovelessness. Such was the general impression he was getting. So fine: let substance addiction take a man like that. He was never entirely all there to begin with. Euthanasia was always his exit, from the get-go. The girl had done her duty, poor thing.

A change of subject visibly crossed her mind as she smiled with a fondness, "Sorry about Billie. Tonight."

Before they'd left the Studio Lot, Billie Ahrsatz, in her tersest tones, had warned Mark that his daughter was officially off the tour now. Fantasy Vacations was not legally responsible for her. All their agreements were null and void. She would be excluded from all further Celebrity Vacation activities and no portion of the Perdues' money would be refunded. The same would go for Bodie and the Lostigs.

"Billie's all right," Mark said. "She's just doing her job. And who knows: when the kids come back to the hotel safe and sound . . ."

"She just legally has to warn you. As soon as they show up, they'll be back on the program."

A lull grew in the compartment again, and the topic of Rod's death saturated right back. Maybe Mark was interested in making mischief of some sort. He asked of Rod's entire problem, "But really *why?*" and for emphasis he reached out and pressed—or tapped—her knee. Touch was allowed in this last hour, because their chastity had been so perfect—and because they were sitting out front where the kids might come by any minute and see them, so they were safe that way—and because this conversation about the AIDS-ridden, bearded Veronica Lodge was so, almost, *ghoulish* it refrigerated any threat of eroticism, in the space of these two bucket seats, with intervening gearshift.

Blythe phrased his question, "Why was Rod so fucked-up?"

She would have to think about that, looking out into the source of coppery light all around the front entrance of the hotel. Dozens and dozens of little lightbulbs, row upon row. She mused, "He had a wonderful family. I love his family. And we're still," her two scissoring fingers tapped together.

She thought for a while. Then, still looking at the hotel entrance, she said, "Poor doorman. He's in there. He's in there with his white gloves, waiting to see if we're going to need help with our luggage or whatever. Wasn't it sharp of the night clerk? To call about Bodie when he left? I don't see the security camera. 'Cause I suppose this is where they got a shot of little old Bodie wheeling his way up the road."

Then she turned to Mark's question, "It's just how Rod was. I guess being so completely a 'user,' or 'exploiter' . . . is essentially a form of being scared to death. It ended up as like a vampire thing: By being unable to love, he got to be absolutely the most lovable guy in the world. Everybody knew Rod. Really. He was everybody's favorite person. He had some kind of *magic*. He really did light up rooms. You know," she finished, tiredly, in the light of her own failure as a human being, "charisma."

Mark blurted out in a sudden whine, while lifting his arms, with an outreach *as if* to embrace her, though still lying back against the car door, "I have the sense, oh my love . . ." That was a forbidden word, but he had no choice, there was no other word, nothing else would convey what he meant to give her permanently, during this little window of time where eternity could be glimpsed. "I have the sense that you are coming out of a long, long, long misunderstanding." There was almost tearfulness in his voice, but not the real thing, only the comical simulation of it. "The sense that you just totally wasted your time."

That was supposed to be *consoling*. This pretty woman, ten years younger than himself, looked at him, for some while, with an evident open-mindedness, making a game effort of revising her life backward. Trying to see it all as a waste of time, and merely "a long misunderstanding."

Misunderstanding of herself, and of Rod. Misunderstanding of love. Misunderstanding what people mean when they speak. *A short unhappy life* was the medical expression, back home, that had condemned the sketchy intrauterine diagram to an early nonexistence: so the thing had been well warned off. Mark was lucky, and *it* was lucky. As for Mark, he himself was "alive," and right now he was grateful just for the sight of Blythe Cress, the djinn of desire before his eyes, she was a candle, her embraceable shoulders unembraced. All he meant was for her to despise her old boyfriend. To feel licensed to go ahead and despise him. Of course he, Mark, was more like the cold-blooded "vampire" at this moment and felt a secret consanguinity with such a one as Rod, whom he shouldn't judge harshly. In this car, *he* was the one with pessimism running in his veins, unsuspected by her, all weekend watching her like an old Peeping Tom, during a little four-day trip in Los Angeles, behind his mask.

She, with her shamed hang of the head, at last on consideration looked slightly thankful to have heard such a verdict on her life: that ten years had been wasted on a misunderstanding, and what a short, unhappy life *she'd* had.

Blinking her eyes at the emerging end of the "tunnel" he'd described, she said, "Well, I'm tired," and she smiled.

EVEN "FANTASY WEEKENDS" have to end. At the front desk there were no messages for him, according to the two kids behind the counter wearing hotel badges. Hotel employees would have no insight into him, naturally; he was just a moving silhouette; they wouldn't see he had cut off an apparently genuine love in his world— nor have any idea he had just conducted such a long, strange conversation, a conversation oddly cruel, oddly shallow on important subjects. Nor care, nor notice him at all. Behind their tall counter, a really good-looking girl and a really good-looking boy in their best clothes for work, they'd been obviously flirting, while they loafed and goofed off together during the long, dull hours they had to kill on their shift in an empty lobby with nothing but soft piped-in music all night and the half acre of purple carpet stretching untracked before them. When he inquired, the girl poked a few buttons on her computer and said there had been no calls to his room. He knew there wouldn't be. He continued to believe Lotta would come back soon. Everything was going to be fine. *His* particular job was not to worry. That is, not to think. Just now in the car, Blythe had tilted her head and smiled and said *I'm tired*, and when she uttered those words, with that smile, it meant he was released into his marriage again. Tomorrow was scheduled to be a busy, event-filled final day for all the young Celebrities. It also meant she didn't necessarily accede to his brutal, oversimple explanation of her time with Rod.

He stood inside the big elevator and let the heavy bronze doors close over his face, and when the floor started swelling fast underfoot, his condemned elevator-stomach (as the illuminated number began climbing heavenward) made him—as he always did in elevators—tally up the ways he hadn't measured up in life. In Karlsruhe, where *he* wasn't present this weekend, the main interest would be whether the new European collider would strike up a Higgs boson. The Higgs boson was the particle responsible, at the beginning of time, for the birth of the illusion of "mass." He was guilty of actually not caring about that, at forty-two. Or rather, he could see it as merely the product of the software designers programming the detection system. They were programming it to find what they thought would be there. So programmers find the thing they're looking for. And don't find anything they aren't looking for. Then, as the elevator kept soaring, he couldn't help but notice a goldfish lying behind him on the carpet in the back corner.

To all appearances it was an actual goldfish, rather than a fake or a toy. And it looked alive, it wasn't dead, it was mostly inert, but every few seconds its gills pulsed. He was positive. He watched it for a while. It lay still. Then, sure enough, its gills gaped again. The dorsal fin flexed.

This was the work of children who were probably guests in the hotel. Or it involved the pranks of older kids. Certainly the fish was not a *passenger* that was going to get off at its own floor, though that was the feeling, an odd fancy he sensed at his back, as he turned away from its corner and faced the heavy bronze doors, his own ghost reflected there, and the rising mausoleum slowed down and sounded its subdued clang, and the doors opened on what must be his floor—all the floors looked alike—(however, he could tell he was definitely not experiencing lymebrain, its disorienting periphery-sizzle; he knew exactly where his room was)—so he left the goldfish to its own fate and turned left down the corridor, toward his room, rather than, say, somehow scooping and flicking the little, cold, flippy thing onto his palm and *carrying* it, carrying it on an open palm down the corridor, to get it into a glass of water. Which is maybe what he ought to have done. Instead he went along as usual, his fingers counting the ibuprofen pellets deep in both pockets.

Those were confusing, hard months, the months before the courses of antibiotics, when he seemed like a hypochondriac and kept getting different diagnoses, the months when the shooting pains and fatigues and finger-electricity and mental lapses and vengeful headaches all entered his life, all as an extremely *educative* new force. He'd been trying to keep it a secret at work but one day couldn't hide a certain fact, that either he'd *never* understood gauge-symmetry models, or else he'd lost his grasp of the subject. It happened during a graduate student's oral exams: in his mind there was only an empty place, a lesion, where the knowledge ought to have been. At least these days the antibiotics had worked, and the time of the terrible symptoms was over, and he had tenure. But still, from that point on, he would always be taking the back stairway in getting to and from his office. And (accidental boon) they would keep him off any real committees.

At his hotel room door, the magnetic-strip card came to hand. With its plastic corner he tapped his own upper lip, then lower lip, then his left cheek and his right cheek. And he tapped the wood above the doorknob, below the doorknob, and to its left and its right. Then he inserted it. He didn't feel the least bit sleepy. He might even have trouble falling asleep. Because he would go on worrying about Lotta. Yes, they both had taxi money and cell phones. Yes, Bodie might be only a harmless poseur. Yes, Lotta was smart. Still, a day will not be finished until Lotta is home safe. That's how it will be, until she moves into a college dorm. Or, sooner, switches to a school in her cousins' place in Connecticut.

Also, he had a longing for Blythe and that, too, would keep him awake. He felt like an eighteen-year-old. Blythe hadn't stayed in the car: she'd gotten out and escorted him to the front door, where there was more talk, just meaningless talk. The doorman wasn't around anymore. Mark did say one thing, in parting. He said that there must be no letters or phone calls between them, nor emails either, that they must never have any contact again.

But the effective point was, a communications blackout would put her in his thoughts perpetually and eternally.

She said, "I know."

So there was nothing to say after that, and like teenagers they stood separated but staring into each other's eyes, just drinking each other in, it seemed to go on for minutes, and did in fact go on for some time, while possibly the hotel's front security cam was watching them. If they were being reproduced on a security screen, they would look very odd: two grown-ups standing, facing each other, upon a threshold, not talking, just staring, in their different heights, she with her heels together, her hands hanging at arm's length clasped before her, with that skeptical flickering light in her eye. His own overfamiliar dowsing rod had been somewhat fattened by that conversation, somewhat lastingly, and indeed, he was still walking around with a nudge of that. It would subside with distraction. As always in hotel rooms, when he came in, he whacked the power button, in passing the TV, and he headed for the minifridge—those being the two cornucopias, rather specious and rather disappointing cornucopias, that furnish the semierotic life of the hotel "guest." On the television, a soothing voice materialized, narrating a kind of slide show, describing a hotel website where the menu of guest amenities might be perused. It's always a too-shallow menu. There is no end, in this life, there's only frustration, only desire. The answer to the question *Why would he want to insult all Blythe Cress's values?* was obvious: damaging her was a form of vengeance, babyish vengeance, for his not being able to sleep with her. Such is the damage people inflict. He couldn't call her and try to fix it. He wasn't the type. Every moment a fossil. In the minifridge he found a kind of cheese spread in a plastic capsule. And crackers. And a bottle of fizzy water. Some bland-looking disks of salami, fanned out inside heavy shrink-wrap. So he sat at the desk and set out the elements of his meal on the desk blotter beside the paper sleeve containing the return-trip airplane tickets, first cracking the seal on the cap of the carbonated water. The label on the bottle displayed an illustration of a tiny mound of colorful fruit, small as a molehill, spilling forward in sunny abundance, including cherries, and a pineapple, and citrus fruit. The bottle's released fume was fragrant as furniture polish. But any real taste turns out to be more in the fumes, rather than in the water itself. The label listed no ingredients, only "Natural Flavors." Among esters it would contain a few parts per million of industrial flavorings, amyl formate, dimethyl octanol, probably some form of butyrate, isoamyl acetate, ethyl propionate.

THE ISSUE OF the goldfish, at last, rose up as inescapable just when he had lain down in bed and turned off the light and pulled up the blankets and made himself comfortable. It either needed to be kept alive in a water glass or be killed—by stepping on it on the bathroom floor or by flushing it down the toilet into septic hell. He really, still, wasn't sure which of those solutions he would go for even as he threw off the blankets—and with annoyance—with a pointlessness foredestined—he went out into the corridor. The likeliest thing was that, by now, it had either died or been rescued. At least fifteen minutes had passed since he'd seen it breathing, but who knows, maybe a goldfish can survive a long time.

No one would be around in the hallways at this time of night. And there was nothing indecent about his flannel pajamas, a newish, not-raggedy set that Audrey bought him for a birthday present, as a joke, because they were printed all over in little illustrations of atoms—the old Bohr model, with electrons buzzing in ovals like horseflies, nothing like the actual Pauli quantum wave shapes, their fierce beauty. Out in the corridor he carried his cell phone with him in hand, in case Lotta might call while he was out of the room. But also, admittedly, a Lyme disease recoverer wants to carry a cell phone with him in a hotel corridor, just in case the Great Mental Incompetence should overcome him in the maze of identical doors and he should need to call the front desk for help. That happened once. It happened at a Chicago conference, but nobody in the Berkeley delegation found out about it and there were no echoes of it.

He pushed the elevator button and stood on the carpet. The possibility was always there, that his not caring about the Higgs boson—or about new gauge-symmetry ideas either—was another Lyme symptom, but an *emotional* kind of late-stage symptom to go along with Lyme incompetence. It would be Lyme *indifference*. In any case, an indifference was a relief. And when the elevator did arrive, it was empty. No goldfish in that corner. No goldfish in any corner. So it was either dead or it had been rescued. The lobby clerks might have rescued it. If it was now swimming in a glass on the rim of a bathroom sink, seeing its own golden reflection in a mirror, it could think its reflection was another little fish—that *is* how their little fishy brains work, organisms programmed to group together in great, flashing shoals and live amidst each other's mirrored behavior—so it might *believe* it was seeing a friend in the glass swimming alongside and might swim onward in that knowledge.

In any case, he didn't worry about Blythe, in consigning her again to the life she'd devised for herself. Downstairs, at the moment of farewell in the doorway, she began explaining one last thing: *Anyhow, Mr. Magoo was a cartoon*, reverting to an earlier topic of the weekend, as she felt compelled to tie up every last loose end, and compelled, too, to seal *him* off in his own preserving anecdote. *He's supposed to be nearsighted. He toddles along and he, like, drives straight off a bridge but gets caught by a ferryboat. Or he falls in a manhole but thinks he's in a movie theater. So he's perfectly happy.* The hotel doorman had vanished, and Mark wondered if the security camera, on closed-circuit screens, was reproducing her lips as they moved. *He's always congratulating himself. Very self-congratulatory. He goes toddling along chuckling about the "nice breeze" while an anvil is dropping right next to him.*

The phone rang in his hand, where he stood in the hotel corridor. It was Lotta's wrongtone. Lucky thing he'd brought it.

"Hi, Dad. Are you back at the hotel?"

"Where are you?"

"Everything's fine," she said, but he could tell everything wasn't fine. "Can you come and get us? Is Blythe already gone home with the car?"

"Where are you?"

"We're by the Hollywood Sign. But we're hard to get to. I'll have to guide you here by phone."

"What exactly is the problem?"

"Bodie's wheelchair fell. He's fine. Everything is fine. He just fell down in this little *place*, and now he's having a little trouble getting out. It's one of those thingies like in deserts. He just needs a rope. Do you have a rope? Of course you don't. You would have to get Blythe to bring a rope."

"What kind of a 'thingie' is he in?" said Mark, afire with satisfaction.

"I guess *gulch* is the word. You know he's incredibly strong and he *would* be able to get himself out. But in this one situation, it's pretty straight down."

Mark was back in his own room now, watching the image of himself in the big mirror, Mark Perdue in pajamas holding a cell phone to his ear—looking always oddly flat-faced or flat-haired whenever he wore pajamas. But he was crowned with happiness. Happiness because

111

this was a *soluble* problem, rather than some sticky or intractable (or "tragic," newspapers would say) situation. And *he* could solve it. He *liked* prolonging the girl's childhood, and he could admit it. In the mirror he watched himself actually frowning in judicious pleasure. Admittedly, too, this provided a reason for calling Blythe. She had looked bridal and hopeful standing before him under the hotel marquee with her hands folded and her heels together.

Lotta in his ear said, "We're out where you can only hike to. You'll have to park down below and I'll guide you here. So call me when you get near. So I better hang up and save the batteries."

"How did you get there? *Why* did you go there?"

"Pilgrimage: Touch the Hollywood Sign. You know the Hollywood Sign? On the hill? Huge tall letters? It's a pilgrimage, because we're 'Big Celebrities.'"

That last sarcastic remark was directed at Bodie's hearing, there with her.

"All right, well, I'll call Blythe. Blythe will know how to get there. And we'll bring a rope, as you suggest."

IT WAS 11:17 at night, and of course Blythe wasn't the sort of person to have a coil of rope, but in Los Angeles plenty of places are going to be open all night, and she knew where there was a big regional supermarket chain store. It was less than a mile drive, a huge place on a parking lot, windowless, tall-walled, a bunker fortified against the coming sieges of the Los Angeles class wars. At the foot of its northern face it invited customers via a limited set of glass doors. The tough, dirty, urban Subaru pulled into a spot.

And they both got out. And went inside like a married couple over the grooved rubber mat together, or really more like young partygoers out for more six-packs of beer, into the confusing light, the heavenly clinical hospital light in the long, bright, empty aisles where pop tunes play all night long. He was experiencing the savor of duplicity. For here in eternity he was pretending to be single again, and young again, Blythe at his side. She had put on different clothes for this outing—faded jeans now—and under a light jacket, a sweater. He would always have his wife, his Audrey, all sewed up, back home in Terra Linda. He might almost take Blythe's hand, or even throw an arm around her as they wandered. But that would have been electrifying to both.

"It can't be just clothesline," she said. She kept a little ahead of him. "It has to be strong enough to hold a big guy like Bodie. Did Lotta describe the problem much?"

"No." All he imagined was that Bodie and the wheelchair lay at the foot of a slope.

"There we are," she said. "Right here."

Native of this town, she'd gone straight to it. In an aisle called Homeware, a cardboard display stood out, holding nylon ropes in transparent shrink-wrapping. The coils were advertised to be 3/8-inch, fifty-foot, six-hundred-pound-test ropes, and Blythe snatched the top one and then reversed direction, to go pay for it, without examining it, leaving him behind, standing at the rope display, foolish, happy, an errant husband, out past his bedtime: he actually found all the plastic and aluminum mops and pans and spatulas on the racks interesting, or just stupefying, just arresting, only because he wished to prolong the dream of shopping together—but he gathered his wits and got going, and he caught up with her. Her artistic hand—small-boned, freckled, rehearsed in the lifting and handling of medieval kimono fabric and samurai costumes, which, she'd said, must be stored flat and spread open in felt-lined, shallow caskets, never on hangers, to preserve them archivally through the ages—passed the plastic rope across to him, while her other hand dug in her jeans pocket at that cute, tender inguinal hollow of the hip. She was pulling out crumpled bills.

Everything is overpackaged. This coil of rope was encased in heavy shrink-wrapping with melted seams, *and* it was girdled by a cardboard band that, alone, would have held it together. The standard recycling emblem, of three arrows chugging around a triangle, chasing each other, showed an SPI resin code of 5, so the strands of the rope would probably be polypropylene. Not the strongest of polymers. The sticker said "$4.99." Surely Bodie Lostig couldn't weigh more than six hundred pounds, even if he were hoisted up *with* his wheelchair.

They stood at the unmanned checkout counter, while their checker—an ultraskinny black girl with her hair in perfect, beautiful cornrows—postponed coming over and checking out their purchase, because she preferred to linger, joking and teasing, with her manager. Tonight in Los Angeles, all the world was flirting. Anybody would think he and Blythe, too, were out together teasing each other. At this point, coming out of the Homeware aisle with their package, they looked more married than dating.

The checkout girl avoided looking at them and went on trifling, dallying, two check stands down, bouncing on her heels, describing something, patting epaulets on her own shoulders, hanging her hands before her, limp as paws. Mark couldn't be patient, because all this while, his daughter and Bodie were stranded in their gulch. He had phoned her from the hotel lobby: when Blythe arrived to pick him up, he'd called to tell her they were on their way; and Lotta had told him they shouldn't worry, things were fine, it was a warm night, and they had a package of Fig Newtons. Still, Mark wanted to get to them. Things could always go further wrong, in various unthinkable ways.

Blythe took this becalmed moment to insert, turning to face him, "You know it wasn't a 'misunderstanding.' I was thinking about what you said."

"What wasn't?" he asked. But he knew.

"The Rod thing. You couldn't call it a misunderstanding." She made a pinching gesture at her eye, as if, with a discerning squint, to adjust a kind of fine monocle: "You *see* the disaster coming. You *see* it all perfectly, but you go through it anyway, in slow motion." She actually gripped Mark's elbow. "That was exactly the awful thing, how we *did* have *no* misunderstanding, not at all, about what we were doing."

He couldn't find a response. She had reproved him. Which he deserved. But she'd made reproof easy. She made it light, and kind of comical; she somehow turned it to his benefit, transforming a stupid insult into a cause for better closeness, going on, "Ah, but," she tapped the coil of rope against her own temple, "for a scientist, everything is a misunderstanding, isn't it?" (She plainly *had* been watching a lot of his old YouTube clips.)

She added, "Or, no: Everything is just 'a mere *understanding*'?" quoting his old stuff more accurately ("A Mere Understanding" was the title of one of the old televised PBS episodes)—and, so saying, she made her eyes glaze over blindly, and her magical palm rose and spread a blesséd unreality over the whole visible store, over all the aisles and checkout stands, everything, the shelved products in their seductive packaging, all the advertised answers to human afflictions and desires, all the wavelengths of color in the range between ultraviolet and infra-red, whose buzz they stood within, a world made of merely human understandings. It was the phenomenal world the unborn boy orbited near, but then veered from, when he was waved off. Mark managed to make a sort of smile, a contrite smile, a grateful smile, she was so generously making herself a student of his old work, Googling things in her free hours.

The checkout girl then, in her chain store uniform, came flounc-ing, limp hands still hanging like paws. She greeted them with maxi-mum gaiety, "Hey, folks," tapping the cash register's keys to waken it, unlocking its money drawer with a key from her smock pocket, "How're you folks doin' tonight?" She was showing a superficial repentance for not having come over right away. Her plastic name tag said her name was Raya. Mark found he immediately forgave her, and was willing to be in love with *her, too,* tonight, promiscuously, though she was probably barely twenty years old and of course had the limitation of living here. Her hair was beautifully and meticulously cornrowed with little candy-like beads, jujubes, woven into tassels, including a thread or two of actual tinsel.

"We're fine thanks," said Blythe, flatly. She was *not* yet forgiving the girl.

"You folks find everything you were looking for?"

She says that to everyone. Their one and only item passed over the glassed-over abyss of the red eye, causing a *bip* sound, and went straight into a plastic bag. "Is this all, for you tonight? Just some rope?"

"That's all, thanks."

Speaking of the rope, she cracked a joke as she handed it across, "Headin' off to a nice lynching? Looks like?" and then she rolled her eyes, because she'd shocked *herself*, "Wooh, I din' say nothin'," she smiled up at the lofty ceiling of the store and laid a beautiful hand on her cheek, which was like the metaphor of a slap.

Blythe saved her, saying, "It's a rescue operation," pulling the rope out of its bag, waggling it, smiling a little—"Rescue operation."

The girl in gratitude laid her two hands upon her throat, and she closed then opened her eyes, then she spun away, to go back to flirting with her manager, bidding them, "You folks have an *excellent excellent* night now," petting and smoothing her own bottom as she restored herself to her true station.

Mark did want to be single again. He'd missed out on all this, he'd missed out on the affinities of night people, the kindling of warmth in the cool Southern California night. He'd gone straight from MIT to Columbia and then the Berkeley job, while here in Los Angeles *all the while* was a world you didn't need postgraduate degrees to get entrance to, or *any* schooling, you just jump in. It was a world where conceivably a person might ask a pretty girl like Raya *When do you get off work*. And she might even take such an offer seriously. She would even know some clubs, at her age, and at this time of night. These people were immortal. They of course might see *him* as awesome (they would imagine him in a lab coat, manipulating formulas, a wizard, his chalk sketching in air), but *they*, here, they were like faeries. Mark, during his time, had missed out on Southern California. Now, married and tenured, and somewhat lymebrained, he would always have missed it. Blythe, meanwhile, was already headed for the exit. He owed all this ease to her, his guide in the city of night, and as they passed out into the dark, he added a little more, to try to explain, walking nearer to her, catching up, because he was going to indulge himself in some additional apologizing:

"I mean, supposing with Rod it were in some sense true—"

True, that is, that Blythe's ten-year relationship with the musician *was* only a big misunderstanding and a waste.

"—Well then," he said, "that wouldn't be funny."

It was already horror enough: Blythe had reached a point of no longer admiring her man, which happens sometimes, but this was while he was dying. As the one person in all creation who knew him best, she'd come to despise the human being she was handing out of this world.

Anyway, outside, his own voice was oddly damped and quieted in the open air. This was a huge city. Everywhere a thrum. Everywhere a freeway overpass's tensile clang. His little, provincial San Francisco couldn't possibly compare. This was a city of the world, a profound

city, an endless city. The windowless superstore really did look fortified against the day when the masses would storm it in food riots.
Here in an L.A. parking lot, as she kept a half step ahead of him, he
watched the woman who, in another life, he might have lived alongside of—the crisp cedar hair shoulder-length, the one shoulder poised
a little higher than the other as she walked, the seat of the denim blue
jeans tailored to possess the famous advertised valentine. The whole
person of "Blythe Cress," of course, made sense here in Los Angeles.
There were elements back home that held *him* together, too. Terra
Linda held him together, its surrounding hills, its freeway exit ramp,
where, right away in the sudden serenity, you hit a stoplight beside
the mall. The University of California held him together—his lucky
assigned parking place on campus, the retirement package—the toll-
booth at the Richmond Bridge every afternoon, and of course Lotta
and Audrey, and the monthly checks to Countrywide Home Loans,
and the necessity soon of repainting the house, according to the pre-
scribed palette of colors allowed by the neighborhood covenants
and restrictions. In a way, one *is* already dead. Already dead-and-
in-heaven, *while* living it all. That was the secret he knew. And that
secret, it too was another thing that had always held him together.
That perspective.

Blythe popped the locks on her Subaru—which, too, he wouldn't
leave his wife for, its sticky drink holder dedicated to *this* woman's
travel mug, its bucket seat dedicated to *her* famous valentine, its rear
hatchback floor burdened with *her* NORTON SIMON MUSEUM gift shop
bag—and as she sorted through her key ring, she said with a gesture
out toward the stranded kids on their hillside, "Coyotes and perverts.
That's all we might have to worry about." She was sitting there stab-
bing her key myopically in the general area of the ignition slot. "And

contrary to the general belief about L.A., the populations of coyotes and perverts here are not that, uh . . ." (*stab stab*) "not that densely concentrated."

The way she dimly, trustingly poked at the ignition, it was fetching, it was seductive, her passivity; this woman's endless mystic *torpor* could take over his male soul. In his heart, everything was revokable. He *was* as already dead, watching all this from an afterlife. And so he was mute, and couldn't speak out, at least not anything of the truth, brimming with it. He, Mark, *he* was the only "pervert" right now, seeing her through his peephole for these three days as a visitor. He was definitely here in Los Angeles in the company of a young woman he could sleep with at will—rather than (*for example!*) home diapering and sedating a baby who is paralyzed, blind, retarded, hopeless. That trade-off—the bona fide legitimacy of it—grants a fantastic buoyancy in the L.A. night in a parking lot, a buoyancy that is an entitlement completely legal and lawful and aboveboard, for a man who has the smarts and the integrity not to literally sleep with her in the end.

★ AT A CERTAIN point she swung a left off Los Feliz, and he supposed they must be getting in the area. "I don't see it," he said. In postcards the Hollywood Sign seemed to loom so large it ought to be visible from all over.

"I actually know a pair of guys. They live right here in Griffith Park, and I could call them if we need a hand. They'd come out. They're devoted to me. But maybe you ought to phone your daughter. Start getting directions from her. Tell her we're just about in the area."

He took out his phone and opened it. Meanwhile he was ducking to see through the windshield toward a dark territory uphill that must be an unbuilt slope. She glanced at him and informed him, "It's not illuminated at night."

So Lotta was somewhere in that void. He hit speed dial on his phone. And she came right on: "Are you here?"

"How's everything going?"

"Oh, it's a party. Except poor *Bodie* is twenty feet down. I've been tossing him Fig Newtons like he's a performing seal, poor guy."

"I think we're nearby," Mark said. The car had come to a stop before something. "There's a sign on a gate: NO TRESPASSING. CITY OF LOS ANGELES. THIS AREA IS NOT OPEN TO THE PUBLIC."

"Those signs are everywhere. Are there any houses around where you are?"

Blythe swept the rope coil off the dashboard and told Mark, "This will have to be close enough." She was getting out of the car. "We'll hike in a little. I think soon you'll be able to shout and maybe hear each other."

Meanwhile Lotta on the phone was continuing, "We got here by this little *road, behind* some houses. It was flat and easy. Do you see anything like that?"

"Oh we should have bought a flashlight!" Blythe cried as she walked away. She ducked through the gate to set out on a dirt road beyond the NO TRESPASSING sign.

"Let me hang up now," he told Lotta. "Blythe seems to know where she's going, and once we've made progress I'll call you again."

Lotta said, "Uh-oh. Dad?"

He had been slightly aware of the sound of a helicopter's rotors.

Lotta said, "They're looking right at us."

"Who, Lotta?"

"They've got a spotlight."

From this back road, no helicopter was visible. Nor any spotlight. But he could hear it. Moreover he could hear it reproduced, sharply, on the phone to Lotta.

"Is it police?" he said.

Blythe, ahead of him on the dirt road, stopped and turned, and she put her hands on her hips, watching Mark's face.

Lotta was speaking to Bodie, telling him, "They wouldn't do that if we were a manzanita bush." Then she spoke into the phone, "Whoa, Dad, they're shining the light directly on us. Whoa."

Blythe, standing there, had begun letting her head loll in discouragement. She told Mark, "The whole place has surveillance cameras."

"I think they're going," said Lotta. "They're going."

Then with a loud *whap-whap*, the helicopter came into view. It must have been hovering above a spot a half mile away, or less.

So Blythe and Mark got going.

His own breath whuffing in the phone as he strode, he could hear Lotta in the earpiece: "They were just having a look at us. But Dad? That was probably a police helicopter, so it's a good thing you're coming. Did you bring the rope?"

"Let me put away the phone now. I think we're near. In a minute, I'll be able to shout for you and you'll probably hear me."

Blythe then stopped him. "Wait," she said.

He told Lotta, "Wait. Don't hang up."

Blythe set her hands on Mark's shoulders, but since touching wasn't supposed to be allowed, especially face-to-face, she kept him at arm's length. "We need to have a little strategy here." She took her hands off Mark's shoulders. "I think I should go back to the car. You have my number on your phone. You—by yourself—should go up and get them. I'm an employee of Fantasy Vacations, I don't want to *be* up there. If you need me, you can call me. Meanwhile, I'll go off and find a couple of friends. I know these two people in Griffith Park. Just in case you need somebody strong to get Bodie out of his gully, these two guys are very athletic, and they're buff, and they're my pals: they'll come out."

"You think I won't get lost up there?"

"It's not complicated up there. And me, I'm an employee of Fantasy Vacations. I don't want to involve them if the police do catch you-all trespassing. I'll be much more useful on the outside of this. So. Better hurry."

Mark just stood there looking at her, trying to show as much self-doubt as possible.

"Take my word for it," she said. "I'm more useful if I don't get arrested."

"Dad, are you there?" said Lotta's voice in the thimble of the phone speaker.

★ ALL HE HAD to do was aim for the place where the helicopter had come out. Throughout the area, the true, original Los Angeles desert here opened up and showed itself, in a dry slope of scrubby little plants, crisscrossed with any number of footpaths to choose from, all braided back and forth. Plainly there was always plenty of hiking here beyond the no-trespassing notices. A flashlight wouldn't have been necessary, because Los Angeles's nightlong orange radiation never fails. The terrain all around was becoming clearer as he rose on the slope—his Berkeley shoes in the pulverized gray talcum— and then a dry streambed of a soapy hardpan, in streaks, white, as if the soil here caked up in fluffy salts, carbonates, $CaCO3$, $NaHCO3$, looking as if he might find it citrus tasting and caustic on the tongue if he pinched up a bit of it. Though he didn't. When he got up on a rise, he stopped, to look downhill and uphill, and orient himself, and he realized that the Hollywood Sign had been visible for some while, a kind of assumption in his mental periphery, looming ghostly in the diffuse orange haze, the tall letters personifying themselves perfectly, just as on TV. Monuments do that: by immense constancy they attain an invisibility. And by invisibility, omnipresence. He took out his phone to try calling Lotta, rather than shouting for her at this point.

Then although he didn't hear the far ringtone in the upper slope, he *saw* the candlelight opening up: it was her cell phone's screen in the distance. Lotta's voice in the phone said, "I see the light of your phone." And he told her, "I see the light of your phone." It was romance. They were two lightning bugs from the backyards of Illinois out here in California. He could pick out a route. Soon he was following the tracks of the wheelchair's wheels in the dust. The land steepened and tossed. It was admirable how Lotta and the wheelchair boy had made it as far as they did, all under their own efforts, probably Lotta pushing and jamming from behind, in her sweater-and-sneakers outfit, while Bodie would have powered himself along by his own grip on the wheel rims. When Mark arrived, breathing hard, he seated himself where Lotta had been sitting—(she had stood up for him, in her flat-footed, sneaker-shod way, to give him the daughter-hug, awkward and lopsided)—and he said:

"Where's the Fig Newtons. I hope you didn't eat all the Fig Newtons." He wanted his daughter and Bodie to know that, while this was a very bad idea of theirs, he wasn't going to make them suffer for it. Always, of the two parents, he'd been the one to spoil Lotta. Whenever he and Lotta's mother disagreed—over, say, the forgiveness of a flippant remark, or the purchase of expensive shoes—Mark was always the lenient one. By the time of her adolescence he had reached a point of finding himself defending the whole practice of spoiling your child, on principle, spoiling her as much as you can, as long as it's still possible.

She asked where Blythe was, and he told her Blythe had stayed down. "She's got the car. I'll call her."

But he didn't get his phone out. He was still out of breath.

"Hey there, Mr. Perdue," said Bodie, reclining at the bottom of the little cliff he'd gone over. Bodie addressed all grown-ups by their surnames, keeping them in their place. At first he'd been calling Mark *Doctor* Perdue.

"I guess you're not injured, there, ah, Mr. Lostig," Mark said.

"No, no, I'm great." He made a little embarrassed flip of the hand, reclining on an elbow, looking uncharacteristically elegant in a tuxedo. Usually the boy seemed to prefer old threadbare T-shirts, which let the virtue of his pectorals and biceps shine through. His wheelchair was down there too, its chrome gleaming in the general diffuse light pollution. He said, "I see you brought the rope. That is most excellent."

In fact he'd forgotten about the rope, but there it was in the dust before him, right where he'd dropped it. Blythe must have thrust it into his hands. And luckily he'd carried it on up.

"I just need a little traction," Bodie said. "I'm in good-enough shape to pull myself up. Right there beside you is a bush with a strong-enough trunk."

Lotta had picked up the rope and was scratching at the heavy shrink-wrap but finding it too tough for her fingernail to break open. So she started digging in her purse. Probably for something to poke it with. She was too young to be carrying a purse. A purse looked all wrong on her. In her red dress and yellow cardigan and her trademark black canvas sneakers, she'd found a way of squatting so as to preserve the gown's fabric. She was really just a tomboy playing dress-up, in a red dress, using her house key now, to stab holes in the shrink-wrap, lifting the package to tear at its seam with her teeth.

"Here's my plan," said Bodie from twenty feet below. Mark couldn't entirely, freely dislike Bodie Lostig. *Not* disliking Bodie Lostig was something that had begun congealing around him at the moment, ten minutes ago on the phone, when Lotta had said she was throwing Fig Newtons down to "the poor guy," and in that expression *the poor guy*, Mark recognized a badge of woman's admiration, and woman's condescension, and so he saw womanliness and authority in his daughter, too, along with the sight of that new, old shape displayed in her red gown. When a female confers the fond honorific *poor* upon a fellow, the fellow has, by that condescension, been admitted to a fraternity, a secret knighthood, but a comical knighthood among all the poor guys, so that even Bodie Lostig, poor guy, could suddenly matriculate toward the status of son-in-law, as they were all, somehow, all playing dress-up, him too, masquerading as Father.

Bodie meanwhile had described his plan. He wanted the rope tied at its midpoint to the manzanita trunk. Then the two loose ends of it would be thrown down to him. He would tie one end to his wheelchair. Then, on the other length of the rope, he would pull himself up, hand over hand, by the sheer strength of his biceps. Once he'd dragged himself up, he could hoist the wheelchair up after.

"Is the wheelchair damaged?" Mark wanted to know—because that would make a big difference in the task of getting him out of here.

"You could drop one of these out of an airplane and it would bounce and be good as new. We'll see how it rolls when I get up there."

Seen from above, the two big bicycle-sized wheels still looked to be mounted straight and true.

Meanwhile, Lotta stood up. She had liberated the rope and was whipping it to limber it up, freely as a microphone cord. "Like this?" she asked Bodie, squatting down at the base of the manzanita.

The boy down in the ditch said to Mark, "I've always wanted to sit out under the stars with a real astrophysicist. Too bad we don't have a minute or two."

"Too bad there's no stars," grumbled Lotta while she tied the knot.

Mark of course wasn't an "astrophysicist," but one grows tired of making such fine-cut little distinctions. He told Lotta, while she worked on the rope, "You were great onstage tonight," saying it for perhaps the fourth or fifth time, tiresomely, but it was a remark that was supposed to bear so much heavier meaning, like how much he admired the whole package, her, the emerging woman, the competence she was showing in simply tying a knot. He was passing the torch, lying back while she did the work. Here they were in this stupid, mistaken situation, and he was simply jazzed to be with her, as if it were a picnic.

She dropped back from the finished knot at the shrub's trunk, kneeling now to face him, and she said, "Dad?"

She was seizing a serious moment.

"Bodie and I don't want to do any of the activities tomorrow. The video shoot, the awards ceremony. We're done. We graduate."

"You don't?"

He didn't mean to sound so crestfallen. Because in fact such a development would be interesting. Dropping out of the Fantasy Weekend seemed not to be a matter of any shame or failure. It was rather some kind of new adventuresomeness of theirs.

"Bodie thinks it's self-indulgent, and so do I."

"While of course we do understand that everybody has the best intentions." So spoke Bodie, from below. He was tying the rope to the chrome frame of his wheelchair, giving it smart little yanks to harden the knots.

"That's right," said Lotta. "We're both thankful! We both know we're lucky that we have parents who did all this for us," she gestured around at the city of Los Angeles.

Lotta never spoke this way. It was something she'd learned within forty-eight hours. "But you know, I'm not so . . . materialistic, Dad."

She broke that news gently and with a soft wince of sympathy. For of course all dads are materialistic, doomed to materialism, all besotted with unevolved caveman materialism. Now by his daughter's decree, Mark was going to be freed from all that. "Bodie and I want to go walking on the shore tomorrow together. That's all we want to do. They rent all-terrain wheelchairs. We can give our poor chauffeurs a day off. These tours for young people who want to be famous, it's all so . . ." she shuddered.

This was a new kind of syntax or grammar for her, literally: she was starting to build her sentences in a whole new way, but she lacked, yet, the complete arsenal of new jargon.

He's a philosopher: so the dark circle of Celebrities at the Studio Lot had muttered, on the topic of Bodie. *He's holy, he's intense*, that was the refrain of the little chorus around the table. Now Lotta was "reordering her priorities" and aspired to be "a humbler person." The impression was, yes, she'd joined a new religion, and Bodie Lostig was its prophet.

"I've got it all planned, Mr. Perdue," said Bodie. He had begun now pulling himself up, by hand-over-hand grips on the rope. "Los Angeles actually does have public transportation. Little-known fact. It actually *has* a light-rail system. And it's *got* wheelchair accessibility out to the beach."

He was an athlete all right, trained in a Shaker Heights high school gymnasium. He was dragging himself up the slope and didn't seem taxed for breath. Neither of them appeared to be embarrassed about any of this. Whatever petting or embracing had happened in the back of their limousine—and however gleefully the scandal had been publicized by their fellow Celebrities—none of it seemed to bother them now. Mark didn't want a pair of errant kids to be ashamed, or remorse-ridden; and he didn't see their shamelessness as any sort of "audacity" or "impudence." He just found it remarkable. It was almost as if, possibly, not much had happened in the back seat of Bodie's limo. That was a real likelihood. Maybe the first report of scandal was exaggerated. Himself, imagining a scene of love in the car, he had no desire to picture exactly how nurselike or charitable would have been the ministrations of his daughter, his brave, good-hearted daughter, upon this merman, her "trained seal" as she'd referred to him, and on the whole it was better for him to guide his thinking away from it. Really, maybe it was true: maybe not much had happened.

"No kidding," said Bodie as he came up level upon the beach of earth beside them to evolve toward equal stature, no longer to be pelted with Fig Newtons. "I do have lots of questions for you about your work sometime, as an astrophysicist."

"You're so strong!" Lotta told him, while she clapped at the dust on his tuxedo jacket.

Bodie said, "I was telling Lotta—though I'm sure you get this question a lot—I want to ask you what everything is made of these days. Underneath atoms and quarks, et cetera, down where you smash up atoms." His fingers strummed in the dust as illustration. "Isn't that what physicists really know? The fundamental thing? Supposedly?"

This inquiry was some kind of challenge. There was almost the repressed grin of defiance, or a leer, or a sneer.

It would be odd if inquiring into his ideas as a physicist should seem more insolent than kissing his daughter.

Uphill above them, there was a motion. It was a flashlight, winking, as it swept a path in the steep scrub. And of course it was in the hand of a policeman. He was picking his way down the slope, taking his time, while above him another policeman waited, holding his ground. Which is probably standard police procedure. Because if, say, something like a gunfight ensues, one of the two partners should be at a safer distance.

THE FIRST THING Mark had the presence of mind to do was call Blythe. While the police were still far above, he turned his back and dialed her to say very softly into the phone that it was just as she'd predicted, the cops had shown up, and she should stay away to avoid getting involved. He would phone her later, as soon as he could. He also told her not to bother with recruiting her two strong friends: they wouldn't be needed; and he hung up fast. She hardly had a chance to respond, except to say "Oh, Mark!" Meanwhile, the one policeman had come shambling down the slope, in an apologetic forgiving kind of way. He was a tall African American, in great physical condition, bulked-up, like one who exercises by lifting weights, but he moved with a middle-aged sedentary man's mincing reluctance to be on a steep slope—to be outside of his comfy patrol car at all—in a uniform dry-cleaned and pressed—his immense feet in polished shoes picking out landing places among the woody shrubs. Before he arrived, Bodie murmured, "Sorry, Mr. Perdue."

His daughter added, "Probably they just kick you out. They don't arrest you."

"Or make you pay a fine," Bodie suggested.

The policeman, holstering his big black flashlight, arrived and began by spreading his palms around in air, "Are you folks aware you're trespassing on private property?"

Bodie Lostig, of Ohio, wearing a tuxedo, spoke up, "We thought it was owned by the City of Los Angeles." He was seated in a seductive bathing-beauty pose for the policeman.

"May I see some identification?" he circulated a finger meaning everybody in the circle should come up with something.

Fortunately Lotta had her purse. She would be able to show her new DMV learner's permit; it was just a folded-up page rather than a real license, but it was something. Mark, as he hauled out his own wallet, felt glad to be just a common lowly tourist, here on his daughter's "Fantasy Vacation."

The policeman examined the documents he'd been handed.

His younger partner, still standing far up the slope, shifted his weight, and folded and refolded his arms. He, too, would rather be back in the patrol car.

The policeman focused on Mark, tapping the face of his driver's license: "Is this you?"

Mark didn't answer. Meaning yes.

He went back to examining the other things—Bodie's Ohio driver's license, Lotta's unfolded sheet of paper.

Lotta put in, "We're really just visitors. All we wanted to do was touch the Hollywood Sign."

This cop had heard that before. "Well, I'm going to have to take you all in."

Mark's little heart attack then did come back, not the thing itself, just the moral idea of it, the melodrama, being a victim of circumstances here. An arrest procedure would take hours. "I suppose there's probably a fine, too," he said. Symmetrically his jaw was applying pressure to each of his molars in turn, alternating between left and right, four pulses of pressure per tooth, four molars on each side. He got to the end of a series before pausing to speak again. "Can you tell me how much the fine is?"

"I have no idea, sir," he said.

That meant for sure there was a fine. Because of course he arrested people for this misdemeanor all the time and he knew the exact figures, but he wasn't allowed to mention any numbers, because it would sound like an invitation to bribery. This whole process, including the release procedures, would take hours. They wouldn't be walking freely out the front door of a police station until daylight.

Mark told his young pals, "I'm afraid we might not make the recording session or whatever. The videotaping."

"No worries, Dad. We never did want to do that."

"Are you able to walk?" the policeman asked the beached merman.

"This is my wheelchair. I'm paralyzed from the waist down."

This cop didn't admit any admiration of the feat they'd accomplished, getting a wheelchair all the way up here. He just called to his partner, without turning away, "Jared? You'd better go bring the car down below. All the way round to Canyon Lake. We're going to have to descend."

His partner—younger, Caucasian—gave a hapless flop of the arms, and then went on standing there, going nowhere.

"Folks? Mr. Perdue? We're going to drive you to Santa Monica. We can't use our precinct here."

He again lifted his voice in the night to his partner, telling him, "Also, Jared, you better radio for a van."

The partner went on going nowhere and doing nothing, just standing there on the slope, stretching his neck muscles by dropping his head to one side.

"According to the terms of the Americans with Disabilities Act, we have to provide incarceration facilities with wheelchair accessibility, and our precinct here *happens* to be doing construction work right now on the accessible cells, so they'll take you in Santa Monica."

"May I open out my wheelchair and get in?" said Bodie. "You'll find I'm pretty good in it and I won't need much help. If the wheels still turn. See, I fell down in there."

"We know. There's cameras all up in here. We saw you go in the hole."

Bodie, fast as a squid, or like some beast specially evolved for propelling itself by its forelimbs, had opened his collapsible chair and slithered up and mounted himself in it, in his tuxedo. Now he looked like what Mark had heard he was: the president of the senior class back home in Ohio; and he actually gave a little speech. "Officer? I'd like to say something. I just want to say you'll find we're cooperative. I understand police deal with unpredictable, violent people. So I want you to know that, in the case of us, you're not dealing with citizens who are resisting what you do. We're totally appreciative of the great service to society you provide. We want to cooperate with whatever."

The policeman was taking a mental snapshot, the picture of the articulate, handsome, golden-haired boy. Then he looked at Mark, while, with one finger, he sketched little triangular diagrams among them—"Daughter?"—his finger tilted to Lotta. Then it tilted toward Bodie, ticktocking between the girl and the boy. And Mark had to nod and shrug, meaning yes, they're friends. They're an item. All three of them confederates in this stupid crime. Which would cost them an undisclosed amount in fines. And some hours in a police station. But oddly, Mark wasn't tired. Rather a pleasant, mean irresponsibility had begun to kindle. It arose from a spark deep inside, a spark that had been born at the moment in his hotel room when (the exact time on the bedside clock face was 11:17) he hung up the phone and left "bed-time" in the dust and started getting dressed again for a night on the town. He *liked* this calamity as it was shaping up. He invited it. He *loafed and invited it*, in the words of a grade school poem that came back to him. He liked its getting worse because none of this was *his* life. These detours could lead to yet further detours, so it felt. And in L.A. he could go on indefinitely getting farther.

★ THE BACK SEAT of a police car turns out to be more posh and squishy than one might expect; and this particular one happened to be clean, and new, so that the situation reminded Mark of the fancy Town Cars they send out from big conferences or TV stations. But a police car turns out to have a few crucial, existential differences from a limo. The cage grid segregating front seat from back, the bare lack of interior door handles: such things remind the passenger of his very *non*exalted condition. The two young police officers (one a female) who rode in the front seat didn't talk. His Lotta, however, beside him, talked unself-consciously and brazenly as if this *were* a Town Car taking them around to one more adventure on their Fantasy trip. "Bodie's really nice, Dad," she told Mark for openers, settling in. "We want to visit each other after this weekend. Me go out there. Him come to San Francisco."

By a daughter's spoiledness, a father can be fortified. In a jam like this, her presence was a good-luck charm furnishing *his* bravery and good cheer; he knew that. A spoiled girl is an attainment, she's money in the bank, here and everywhere, magically promising a comfortable decline for himself in his old royalty. The indulgent streak first came out in the case of a certain pink electric guitar. When she was five she set all her desires on a small electric guitar with a pink finish, which she'd only *seen* from the passing car, in a shop window on the way to day care every day. It turned out to be a real, actual, working guitar, not a toy at all, though half-sized. And cost two hundred dollars. Her mother disapproved, with vehemence. She was even too-quickly resentful of the idea, saying—and she was making a valid point—that Lotta's little fingers couldn't yet begin to play it, and she'd probably end up leaving it out in the dew—but Mark went out and bought it anyway. Audrey was stunned, and importantly betrayed. The outcome was, Lotta never touched the pink guitar. It never once came out of its little curvaceous case. Having won it, she put it in the closet and never needed to even look at it again.

Mark turned to Lotta, "Well, yes, may I ask about him, in general?"

Bodie had been taken in a separate police van—one that could accommodate wheelchairs in the manner required by regulations—so Mark and Lotta were alone together for this trip to a Santa Monica precinct, to be reunited with him there. Mark began by inquiring, "He seems awfully self-confident. That is, he seems awfully self-assured."

It wasn't meant to sound critical. All he meant was, obviously, the boy stood out like a *brochure* for a well-adjusted, impressive, ambitious young man. He was thinking for example of that patronizing little speech he'd given the arresting officer. Mark just wanted to get to the bottom of that personality. Find its wellsprings.

Lotta, sensing criticism, didn't answer but stared out the window.

"What exactly is his medical condition?" He was aiming to set an example by speaking lower than she had, within the hearing of the two cops in the front seat.

"Yes, isn't he strong?" she cried. "When he pulled up the wheelchair?"

It was true, as he hauled the rope, his bicep was like a grapefruit inside the cheap tuxedo fabric.

"Bodie's amazing, Dad. He's got his own car at home, and he does all the mechanical work on it himself. He put hand controls on the steering-wheel part, for brakes and accelerating, so he could drive without needing his feet. But he got rid of it. He sold it. Because of the environmental thing. And now he's building himself a quadricycle!"

"Yes, Bodie is amazing," said Mark.

There was not the slightest slant of sarcasm there, absolutely none, but she discerned it anyway; and by way of scolding her father, she said, "If we can ever get out of this mess tonight, he and I still plan to go walking upon the shore together."

Not the beach but "the shore." And "*upon* the shore." There was a whole new pretentiousness at work tonight in his sixteen-year-old, which, however, struck him as a not-bad development. Not at all. A pretentiousness was a kind of first blossom.

"Let us just defer making any decisions about tomorrow, Lott. If we *can* get out of this, there's going to be food and some sleep first."

"You can rent wheelchairs that are all-terrain right here in L.A. with big yellow balloony wheels. He showed me an Internet site. They're like space-vehicle rovers, so you can go out on the beach. Or wherever! And really, Dad, this kind of entertainment-business fantasy, it's toxic to the soul. It's egoism." She had turned on him, though restrained by seat belt and handcuffs, and she carried on, talking in this spiritual vein, so garrulous, the girl who never spoke around the house, who was so determined to get away to Connecticut that the only sign of her presence at home was the firmly closed bedroom door. In Connecticut, she was of course fleeing not just her own social failure at school. She was fleeing home, the waiting area their five-room semidetached condominium had become. Mark sometimes got the irrational feeling she *knew* he didn't really understand gauge symmetry and was avoided in the department corridor, knew by her inborn radar, the ovarian radar, not the specific facts, just the doom in his aura when he came in the door at night from his Berkeley commute. At this moment in the police cruiser, hoping to keep her talking as if they really did have a rapport, it felt like trying to sustain her on a bicycle: he could only watch in suspense. As she went on, she made eye contact with him, for a longer period than ever in her life, or at least ever since she'd become a beautiful young woman. Finally, having denounced and reprehended all the self-centeredness in modern society, she subsided back in her corner of the police car. "How much better just to walk upon the shore."

"Does he, like . . . practice a faith or something?" he asked recklessly.

"Bodie?"

How to begin sketching himself out of this?

"Well, there's a kind of philosophical, ethical . . . *atmosphere* I'm sensing around Bodie."

But he was onto something: it was, yes, precisely the look of a convert or devotee, the just-massaged look, the just-anointed look.

"You see that! You notice that!" She was so pleased she bounced to face him again in her deep-upholstered seat, limited by the seat belt, which had been so ceremoniously applied by the attending female cop, who was extremely careful never to come in physical contact with her at any point in the process. She glared at her father evaluatively for a minute. "You know, Dad, with Bodie's obvious situation," she shrugged toward the fact of the boy's inert legs, "he has really had to face some things." She spoke with a leaden solemnity: the point was, Bodie had faced things Mark had never faced.

She sat deeper back in the seat. As a courtesy the police had released the prisoners from the behind-the-back cuffs, so they could sit more easily with hands cuffed in their laps. Nevertheless, father and daughter were riding along together in actual manacles. Maybe years from now it would be something they would be able to joke and reminisce about, about the time they'd been arrested and booked together as a father-daughter team, trespassing on the grounds of the Hollywood Sign. The arresting officer—the African American one, whose name was McCuddy—said the entire arrest procedure was required by law, including "detainment," and including "determination of arraignment," which must be how they extract the fine.

He ought to call Blythe. He still had his phone.

The thought of calling home—and telling Audrey—had crossed his mind. But that was a different world. Audrey would be asleep. She would have spent the evening on the couch switching around from CNN to the History Channel, from PBS to Animal Planet to Comedy Central, while, in her tall, cylindrical glass of black beer, the band of beige foam collapsed and soapily clung. By now she would be in bed.

So instead he would call Blythe. At the jailhouse they might take away his cell phone. Or even make him empty his pockets altogether. At this point they'd been patted down, but nothing had been taken away, and he was able, with both chained-together hands, to get out his phone.

"But," he went on, "Bodie has some kind of systematic '*program*,' though? He's an environmentalist? In some thoroughgoing way?"

"Oh, it's complicated. He believes we're always constantly committing crimes against humanity. We should sit down seriously some day," she warned her father. This apparently wasn't the moment for serious talk: she turned her attention and watched the street go by.

But then, anyway, she plunged straight into it: "Like for instance, ideally in a perfect world, there wouldn't be packaging. Packaging is just *one* aspect! Packaging alone is some huge percentage of global warming. It's disgusting, the packaging industry during this past century. The packaging industry got way out of hand." (This was the new syntax taking root. It so impressive Mark found he was sitting back and turning over the controls.) "Did you know that beer distillers will have, like, two different can designs—like one brand of beer will be called, like, "Schlumpf," and it's for fat, lowbrow guys, and the other is called "St. So-and-So Lager," and it's for high-class snobs—but the same beer goes in the two cans. It's the same beer. Literally from the same big vat, like in Milwaukee or someplace. So really, the consumer is just buying a label. He's buying a self-image for himself, high-class or lowbrow. They're selling us ourselves. That's what we're buying. A self. By holding a package. By holding a package design in your hand, you get a self. It doesn't matter what's *in* the package. People only want a label. Label for *themselves*. And meanwhile the oceans are dying."

Bodie Lostig had been instructing her on many topics. Maybe he wanted people to bring Mason jars to the store and scoop things out of bins. It was a delight seeing her run through the whole speech.

He ventured, "What's the 'crime against humanity' though? If you're just buying beer."

She sighed in admiration of Bodie, "Oh, he's got this whole *thing*. Ideally, nothing would leave people's property, ever. And almost nothing would be *purchased*, or *bought*, to come *on* the property. Ideally, people would do a little agriculture at home. And fix their own stuff, instead of buying new. In Shaker Heights everybody has big yards, and every house could grow vegetables and have a goat and a few chickens and even their manure could stay on the property. He founded an organization called S.T.O.P. It stands for Stay On the Property. Because every time an American buys something or flips a switch, something dies. Something dies out there in the world."

As she spoke she kept watching Los Angeles go by. Storefronts. Mongolian barbeque. Tanning salon. Discount women's shoes. Nobody here was going to start staying on his own property all day. To feed the goat. And do the laundry in a tub.

Lotta had started frowning. "I don't know. Bodie's father says he's Baha'i, supposedly. Since you ask. Whatever 'Baha'i-ism' is. But Bodie's *father*—" her tone indicated a blanket contempt of the father.

In any case, Baha'i-ism wasn't it. Baha'i-ism had nothing to do with what was wrong with Bodie.

"So, sweetheart, I guess, then, this all explains why he eats so simply? Why he eats raw vegan food? Because cooking it causes global warming and coal mining and oil wars and deforestation."

He sounded derisive, unintentionally. But Lotta didn't seem to notice. Her mind had flown to new things, and she watched the boulevard go by, the rhythm of passing streetlamps, endless shops and restaurants.

None of this was going to the heart of Bodie's mysterious humorless zeal, his unusual rectitude or self-certainty—or fanaticism—or whatever it was inside him compelling that angelic vigilance of his, from his perch. Lotta, looking out the window, observed, "He and I haven't 'discussed' Baha'i-whatever." She turned. "But you know what he does do? Which he *does*? He does his little weekly meetings for people whose parents are drunks. He goes at least every week. His father is an alcoholic."

The constantly evolving Bodie. Now Mark had to picture him in a suburban Cleveland church basement, wheeling in to take his place for an evening, among the folding chairs. Those organizations are themselves religions. "So this would be his—" Mark patted his own heart area, with manacled fist "—his 'inner voice'?"

"His father is such an alcoholic he's irresponsible, and he lies, and he screws around with money. So Bodie grew up with *that*. He says having a weak father is the best thing that ever happened to him. Because it made *him* mature."

"How awful for him," Mark conceded, in a slightly singsong tone, begrudging Bodie a little actual heroism.

"Well, his father isn't '*violent*.' Like he doesn't '*do*' anything. He just has a series of schemes that never work out."

"What does he do? For a living?"

Lotta reflected, despondent. "He's just rich. And drinks and makes promises. I think he's just rich."

So, if the Lostigs were still planning to fly out here, Mark wouldn't anymore have to picture himself confronting a leather-jacketed car salesman with an expensive wristwatch. Instead it would be an amiable lush. Easier to take, limper of handshake, probably letting his wife do the talking, his eyes wandering.

Meanwhile, the cell phone still lay in his handcuffed hands.

It would be a violation of procedure, surely, to make a call now, after the legal moment when he'd been informed he was under arrest. But the phone might be confiscated at the police station. The words *incarceration* and *detainment*, both, had been used in conversation with Officer McCuddy. He'd better try to call while he still could.

"Interesting!" he remarked, of Bodie's whole ethical construction, while opening his phone, "But I think I ought to try this, just for a second." He dialed Blythe, and she answered right away:

"Where are you?" she said. She was in her car, he could tell.

"They're taking us all the way to Santa Monica. Different police station."

"It will be two in the morning or something. And all you had was a little sashimi."

"I'm fine. I made a snack for myself out of the hotel minibar. But listen. Could you get together a few hundred dollars in cash? I'm sure we'll have to pay a fine. I think they'll put us in a cell for a little while, while they process our . . . 'case.' And then make us pay a fine."

"Oh, Mark. After all this, let's get breakfast. Champagne mimosas."

He told her, "I'll get to my own bank in the morning and pay you back. Better make it a couple thousand dollars. That should be more than enough. I'll probably have to pay for three fines: me and both kids. I think they give you a court date, like six months out. And then make you *pay* bail and then you have to *forfeit* bail," he said. "Anyway. Sorry. I'm complaining."

"I'll figure out where the Santa Monica police station is. And drive out. You know, it's not a long drive to Santa Monica. You were already near there. It's really right next to you."

"Anyway," he said. "Gotta go." Into that terse goodbye, he put as much tenderness as he possibly could, with his daughter listening. "I think it's against the rules for me to be calling you."

So he put his phone away, without the cops' seeming to notice. Maybe they didn't care. He was getting the sense this was a minor infraction and they were low-security prisoners.

But Lotta now had been watching him. With a certain expression. Then hidden it, looking back out the window.

She knew. More than suspected. Knew. Her intuition had told her. She knew that he and Blythe shared a liking. And an understanding.

Possibly she'd known for some while—while this silly Vacation was running its three-day course—that the axis of her father's turning world had been budged, just a little, just for one weekend.

But there was nothing in particular she would do with this knowledge. She'd always been a discerning, sharp-eyed child, from her earliest consciousness and her earliest manipulativeness. She was probably even—yes, indeed! she would be!—*amused* by a father's unlikely sentimental adventure. Lotta wasn't merely a sharp-eyed person, she was also a judicious person, capable of discretion, and a merciful and wise person, too—and cagey, too—as sometimes the exercise of mercy and wisdom takes that form, of caginess.

THE NEW, MODERN Santa Monica police station wasn't busy at all. Entirely the opposite. All the action—the handcuffed quarreling whores, the car thieves, drug addicts, bellicose drunks—must be somewhere in the back of the building, or in some other wing, because out front, Mark Perdue and his daughter seemed the only threats to society in all Santa Monica, at least so far tonight—he in his Berkeley attire of khakis and shirt and jacket, Lotta in her red dress, yellow cardigan, and black canvas sneakers. The only assumption anyone could make about them was that they were, plainly, father and daughter, rather than, say, procurer and streetwalker. But there was nobody around to make any assumptions. The place seemed unmanned, or running on autopilot. Overhead lights in the front receiving area came on only from the activation of a motion detector, after they'd all been buzzed in through two doors, under the watch of closed-circuit cameras, their upper arms in the formal, gentle grips of their escorts. The front counter wasn't occupied. It looked, in fact, never-occupied, not even since the day it was constructed and installed according to the architect's drawings and in conformity with all building codes—empty of all friendly clutter, not even a pen or a blotter, except for a large outmoded computer, turned-off, dusty, one more piece of equipment owned and neglected by the city of Santa Monica, or Los Angeles County, or the state of California. Society builds infrastructure for itself—it issues municipal bonds, it hires architects, and it puts up a big new state-of-the-art correctional facility, complete with an efficient workstation out front—then people move back anyway to the back room or loading dock where they can smoke, talk, hang out, put their feet up.

The one cop said to his female partner, "They'll want us to put them in Large Meeting."

Maybe this new part was an annex to the main jail. Meanwhile the handcuffs were coming off. Mark rubbed each bare wrist, though the cuffs had been no discomfort, light plastic. A guard appeared from a heavy doorway, wearing a black T-shirt and jeans rather than a uniform, holding a key that was leashed to his belt, and he spoke into the two-way radio on his waist. "Two in Large Meeting."

The voice inside his belt-radio answered with something like *Will we book them?*

That's what Mark heard. Was it possible that they *not* be "booked"? It seemed a good thing, if there was some unsureness about that. Being "booked" is probably what you don't want.

In any case, the guard didn't respond to the voice in the radio. He ignored it. He ducked behind the counter to come up with two wire baskets, and he held them out, telling his prisoners, "Shoes, belts, contents of your pockets, wallets, all jewelry, purse."

So they complied, side by side, guiltily, including shoe removal, he and Lotta yoked together now by this ceremony. The justice system does make you feel undiagnosably vile as you surrender your shoes and your pocket change. And pull off your silly bangles. Lotta said, while she applied ChapStick before giving up her purse, "I am so sorry about this, Dad. Really." She was trying to be blasé, but the situation had begun to scare her, he could recognize it in a rawness in her complexion, a fixed avoidance of the eye.

The guard said, referring to their belongings in the baskets as he set them aside, "I'll have something for you to sign."

His key opened the door to the next room, which had been visible through a large picture window. It was a bright, linoleum-floored place with plastic chairs and a table.

"That's the camera," he pointed to a recessed box, mounted at the intersection of walls and ceiling. "Try to stay out here where it can see you. If you go over in the corner, you're off camera: somebody'll come in and tell you to move back."

Before leaving he added, "Y'ain't g'be fingerprinted, photoed, or frisked. Y'ave to wait now a few minutes."

And he left them there, in the room called Large Meeting.

So society's slow-swinging door was closed upon them, with a sound of heavy magnets clamping in the electronic latch mechanism. Back out in the entry room, visible through shatterproof glass, the two patrol officers were tearing forms off their clipboards, painstakingly, to keep them ripping exactly along the perforations. That last piece of information—about fingerprints, etc.—seemed to imply that they *wouldn't* be "booked." Booking probably involved precisely the fingerprints and mug shots. It was possible that they were being treated with unusual leniency or even courtesy; their original arresting officer, whose heavy brass name tag pin identified him as MCCUDDY, had seemed an understanding sort; and Mark *had* explained to him that he was only out there trespassing in order to rescue the two children, that he hadn't been trying, himself, to make a pilgrimage to touch the Hollywood Sign. He and McCuddy, while they waited for a van, had conversed a little, about the perils of tourism, and about their respective families and the foibles of youngsters, and about smog. Maybe McCuddy sympathized with a visiting middle-class guy, and maybe he had somehow influenced their fate in the channels of arrest procedures. He and Lotta hadn't been put in "cells," and to all appearances, they wouldn't be thrown in with the brawl of the general prison population on a Saturday night. This room, which they called Large Meeting, was about as gemütlich as a jailhouse could possibly be allowed to be—if harshly lit—its block walls painted a cheerful yellow, its linoleum floor furnished with molded-plastic chairs too light and soft to be wielded as weapons and too durable to be broken up for makeshift knives. There was one table, large and indestructible, with legs as fat as logs. In this room, the most resourceful malefactor in the justice system wouldn't be able to work much mischief, especially as there was no privacy: a big picture window displayed the entire outer entry area, its empty desk and counter. On the opposite side of the room was a low pane of mirrored glass that must serve as an observatory from the neighboring room.

So they might get off light. Their detainment might be finished in an hour, involving a few bureaucratic forms only, and paying a fine. And Blythe in her Subaru was, at this moment, churning through the empty L.A. streets toward them with an envelope of cash.

Meanwhile Lotta examined her reflection in the mirrored-glass observation window. It was set so low in the wall, she had to dip her knees to see herself. She plucked her sweater out in places. And she messed up her hair, scrubbing it around.

The chairs were the stackable sort, with armrests, and Mark took a seat. This predicament was going to offer a kind of opportunity: for an hour or so, he and his elusive, evasive daughter would be obliged to converse! His pleasure in, simply, being with his sixteen-year-old was in some way pathetic and craven, floored as it was by the open space of darkness unprobed, the rest of his life. "Anyway, Lotta, are you serious?" he began. "Do you really not want to show up for the videotaping tomorrow?"

"Tomorrow is today," she pointed out, watching her reflection, while she lifted tresses and flicked them.

With both hands she got her fingers deep into her hair and crushed it in her fists, then began flicking at tresses again.

"What caused the change of heart about Celebrity Vacation?" he inquired. "You and Bodie are, like, 'going AWOL.'" He spoke as if that were a lovely new development. Which was how he did tend to see it. Hearing that Bodie was only an environmentalist had perhaps created a more comfortable border around that expansionist personality.

Lotta, in response, turned and looked at him with an expression meaning there was so much to explain about the world, and so much that was woeful, she couldn't even rightly begin. Then she turned back to the reflective glass and, unhappy with the outcome of her grooming efforts, flopped down in one of the white plastic chairs in a teenage girl's total dejection, inclining her head. "I wish he would get here," she said.

They'd been warned that Bodie's van would take longer.

Then she started to address his serious question. "Bodie has a philosophy. Now don't laugh." Her eyes flashed.

He hadn't the slightest impulse to mock, and it was a sharp pain to him, a fatherly pain, to think Lotta could ever imagine him laughing or mocking. He could have almost opened his mouth to tell her so. A better, readier man would have.

"He has a whole complete thing." She leaned forward. She put her elbows on her knees and pressed her hands together: it was a posture like an athlete on the sideline bench. This was new, for her. Einstein used to say thinking is partly a muscular process—that the *body* is involved in thought—and now here was Lotta looking deliberative, as she never had.

She said at last, "It's all about crimes against humanity *and* crimes against nature. And you know, really, it's the truth." Her one hand actually enclosed the other fist in a gentle washing socket. "Everything *is* a crime, if you just think about it."

She didn't look up, as that announcement would require plenty of explanation, and plenty of deep thought, for a while. She hadn't meant it to come out so flatly. All the while, the one hand kept soothing its clenched opposite. Her feet in yellow footie socks—normally all a-twiddle—had fallen into stillness while she pondered this truth, that "everything is a crime."

"Like, for example," she said. "The amount of jet fuel it took for Bodie's United Airlines plane from Ohio," and she went on about how much fertilizer that fuel might have made, for a Pakistani village to grow rice. Or a microloan might have been offered to some woman who could buy apricot trees. Mark was confirmed in relief. All that was worrying her was the fate of the Earth, that trifle. "And for *my* plane," she went on, "to come down from San Francisco. So we could pretend we're famous. And ride around in stretch limos with fake paparazzi. Did you know, for example," she was quoting Bodie verbatim now, "that just one tankful of ethanol in your car uses up enough corn that *one human being* could have lived on for a *year?* One tankful?"

"Well, does he want to hitchhike back home?" He didn't mean to sound flippant. He was just glad this anguish was only her personal drama, of her own good-heartedness. "I only mean to say, darling, that it's hard for one idealistic individual to change the system and save villages."

"Even just to walk upon this floor . . ." There again was the new preposition, *upon*, and he loved his daughter with such a sharp pang he worried how the world would treat her, even over there in Connecticut, once she'd made her getaway. "When you put your foot upon it, you're walking on a tile which some poor little guy—probably of *some* racial group—in some factory!—was underpaid to make, and doomed to die at a young age, from inhaling the toxic substances in the factory. Or that policeman! Dad, he's black!" she pointed back toward the scene of their arrest. "His grandparents were slaves. And now he has to stand there listening to you talk about 'Celebrity Fantasy Weekends.'" She shuddered, it had been so mortifying, hearing him make idle conversation. "And like the ground our own house is built on, stolen from indigenous people. And the shoes I'm wearing, my Converse All Stars," she inclined her head in the direction where her wire basket had gone, "were manufactured in some *place*, like *China*, in some *factory* by some *woman* probably, where the pollution makes babies deformed and causes the biological death of the oceans and blah-blah-*blah-BLAH!* All so I can cause jealousy! All so I can create jealousy in other people! That's the point of it. Creating jealousy wherever possible." She held her arms up, out from her sides, because her body was sticky from the great swamp of crime she'd been born to wade through, all her life, crime against humanity, crime against nature, perpetrated on her behalf, so she could wear her red party dress. "I am the problem. I am. Do you know we could've had solar panels on our roof ten years ago? And never wreck the lives of Nigerian tribes? Where the oil fields are? Not to mention the poor Iraqis *or* the sea-squirt population."

"Dear heart, we've had this discussion," he said. Her concerns were so sweet, and, in a paradox, selfish. She'd pulled her feet far back under her chair, withdrawing them.

He said, "Remember, Lott? Solar panels would mean cutting out the big sycamore with the swing."

She used to love the swing: it was the one instance of his being a good fatherly handyman and building something for her, long ago when she was little. She still did love it. Only recently this spring she'd sat in it by herself making up songs, with a notebook for lyrics, her toes dragging back and forth in the worn dust. She told him, with wide eyes, in a soothing, healing, even motherly tone, "Fuck the old sycamore, Dad. *And* the old swing. Instead we kill brown people in faraway places." Then she flopped back in her chair, spreading her legs in a way that would have been very unladylike if that dress hadn't been a long one. She went on, "Everybody already knows all this. People go, 'Yeah, wouldn't it be great if everybody did the right thing. Too bad they don't.' Well, why not just *do* the right thing, instead of just saying everything's 'too bad.'"

A child's using the *f*-word, before her parent, is a calculated form of histrionics ordinarily, but at this moment he found, in his own sixteen-year-old daughter, he admired such language as magisterial. At least she would make her way in the world, spoiled girl.

She added, "We still don't have those energy-saving lightbulbs. Putting in *a single one* of those bulbs saves enough energy to—" She shrugged. Feed some village.

"Well, your mother—as you know—she likes it when you flip a switch and you get nice light. It's an aesthetic thing with her. The spectrum you get in those fluorescents . . ."

"It's *so* easy for you. For some of humanity, it's now life-and-death situations. For some of humanity it's no joke. Do you know that? They actually fucking die? Literally die? Fucking die? For a large part of humanity?"

Annoyance had begun to peck. Here he was now in the position of quarreling. Here he was defending society's unforgivable sins, *guilty* of those sins, supposedly—and meanwhile they were sitting in an actual jail, waiting to pay a big fine, a fine incurred by her. He wondered whether he ought to make a little inquiry: how many hungry villagers somewhere might be fed on the, probably, s*everal hundred dollars* of forfeited bail money? A father's ability to take pleasure in having a "spoiled daughter," viewed objectively, is perhaps not necessarily a great life achievement; objectively it could be merely a big mistake, a mistake of a father's own laziness and pusillanimity so the result was, she would grow up to be a selfish, unfeeling woman, *bitchy* would be the current word, and nobody will want her as a wife, everyone will discern it a mile off. Only guys in wheelchairs, with their reduced expectations, will put up with her.

He snapped, "So this is all Bodie's point of view, I suppose."

"Everybody is trying to be *cool*, in American society. And everywhere, too. Everybody is so cool. Everybody is so 'impressive.' Which just belittles everybody else. That's all it is. That's all it is, when you're impressive. You just climb up on top of other people. On other people's right to happiness. You belittle other people. That's how your raise yourself up. Be cooler. Have better stuff. I would really rather live in a tin shack. Really. And eat other people's leftovers. No kidding. That's no 'hyperbole' just to illustrate. I would rather. It would truly be better. Wear crap and eat people's garbage."

He might have thought announcing such an ambition must be the climax in her tirade. Because where could you go higher? But then she went higher. Her fingers took a pinch of the fabric of her own red dress, and she whined, "I'm supposed to make myself look . . ." she shuddered. "Yeah, I won't even say." So she aspired to be like a nun now and cover any beauty. Or dress like Muslim woman, in the total black package. And take vows of poverty, too. "I don't *want* to be superior. Why would I want to be better than anybody? Why would anybody want that? What's so wonderful about having other people be lower down and envy you?"

Mark hardly knew where to begin. The dress came from one of those places where they sell old, used clothing and call it "vintage," so, about that dress, she needn't feel materialistic. In fact, she couldn't honestly feel the least bit materialistic, or guilty about it, not in her heart. In her heart, a healthy acquisitiveness throve. She, in her suburb, at the malls, was plundering the manufacturing base of third world nations with imperial-colonialist lawlessness. She was, tonight, only ashamed. Ashamed of causing all this legal trouble, ashamed of having been caught kissing the paraplegic drummer, all the calamity that unravels around you because your beauty naturally leads to things.

He wanted to get her home. Get her out of this whole Southern California environment, and get her back home where she would again just be Lotta-in-her-pajama-bottoms-and-T-shirt with her cute, blubbery midriff showing. Back home where she wasn't onstage all the time, and where she liked to make herself cucumber sandwiches and commune with her computer behind her closed door. Back home where she might forget that she'd glimpsed a little bond of love between her dad and the media escort Blythe Cress. Maybe that glimpse of a father's unfaithful yearning, back in the context of "home," would be dissolved, forgotten, and even seem like a dream, pertaining only to this bizarre fugue time of Three Days and Two Nights in L.A.

"Did you know Mom had an abortion *before* she was married? I shouldn't even be alive?" Her hands rose, and they cast a disappearance spell up and down her own body. "Rightfully, I shouldn't be here."

"I see. You probably shouldn't be taking up space a third world villager could have used?"

At last he'd begun to tingle with the accumulation of insults.

The fact was, Audrey had never mentioned it. Never mentioned an undergraduate-days abortion. Not in all these years. Of course he'd never thought to ask. Who would think to ask? "Did your mother tell you that?"

"So there should've been another person instead of me. In the normal, rightful course of events, there's no such thing as Carlotta Perdue. 'Carlotta Perdue, Big Star.'"

"Genetically, that's not how things work, sweetheart. You're you. There's always going to be a 'you,' Lotta."

He wanted to slow things down and speak more softly, and get a sense of the new facts underfoot. He'd never inquired about Audrey's sex life before marriage.

And of course didn't *want* to inquire about her sex life before marriage—but it would be normal for a young woman during her college years, who was good-looking and sociable, it would be normal to make some reckless mistakes and need to terminate a pregnancy. His feelings weren't hurt, if she hadn't mentioned it. It probably *wasn't* any business of his.

Lotta, knowing what he was thinking, said, "Mom told me during the time we were discussing what to '*do with*' Noddy."

She was watching her own fingers as they buttoned the yellow cardigan, its many little pearly buttons, all the way from bottom to top.

And then he saw it all. Her wheelchair friend was encouraging this. And it was some kind of fundamentalism. There was always something obdurate and fundamentalist in Bodie, in his exemplary manners and his perfect probity, something evangelical. There's a certain unmistakable clarity in the gaze when people have simplistic views. Now this was all closing in. Now he was up against something not quite human anymore, but rather an *idea*, like a virus. Or rather an "*ideology*."

The father was Baha'i. But one's impression is, Baha'is are blandly "liberal" and so probably lenient. On the other hand, the whole Baha'i thing is somehow a little Islamic-looking, or Islamic-derived: they might be old-fashioned on reproductive issues.

"Tell me about the Lostigs. What's his family . . . do?" But he'd already asked that.

Lotta looked up at him from the project of painstakingly, grievously, buttoning her sweater. "I'm trying to say something here, Dad."

"Ah. I'm sorry, darling. What were you trying to say?" As his tone of voice had grown testy, he had the sense of being eavesdropped on, under the eye of a closed-circuit camera in the corner. These four yellow walls had probably heard a lot of quarreling. This was a tank for people who had made stupid mistakes. Life-changing mistakes. On Saturday nights just like tonight. No doubt some hard words had been spoken here. No doubt these linoleum tiles were, sometimes, a kind of threshing floor. Where people got sorted out. Or sorted *themselves* out. Or, sometimes, failed to sort themselves out. And so, having failed to sort themselves out, would go further on into the system.

He went ahead with the hard question: "You think something else should have been 'done with' the embryo?"

She looked unfairly attacked, lifting her eyes to him, then return-ing to her sweater buttons, grumbling in an evasion, "Well, in the third trimester he's hardly an embryo."

"I think possibly your friend Mr. Lostig has a lot of advice for you on this," he said.

She said as good as yes, by not answering, keeping her eyes on the bottommost sweater button, which in her fingers kept winking in and out of its buttonhole.

He saw now the obvious thing he'd already half realized: the young Mr. Lostig's condition was supposedly a defect from birth, so he tells people *he* might have been aborted. Now he's got the grateful-to-be-alive gospel.

She said, "The truth is, Dad, you're not supposed to get what you want in life, or be the Big Winner. The Big American Beautiful Winner. So other people can be losers."

She might almost be a stranger, with her new rhetoric. Maybe if seen in a positive light, a new anti-abortion thinking could at least give a father cause for a certain hope. If she took fertility so deadly seriously, it might cause a little prudence. It might encourage a little birth control.

Eyes still downcast, she phrased Bodie Lostig's golden rule more fully, "If you're satisfying your desires and *getting* what you want, then that's a wasted life. That's a life in delusion."

All this time she was watching her knee with a glazed detachment.

The word *delusion* was a new one. It added a Buddhist chime to all this, coming via Shaker Heights all the way from Dharamsala. Maybe it came from Ohio church basements, in those weekly meetings, among those folding chairs, in groups where you get to stand up and tell your own sorry tale of woe, after having first acknowledged (it would prob-ably be "Step One") that there is a Power greater than ourselves.

Mark said, "Tell me, is your friend antiabortion?"

She glanced up. She behaved as if she'd never heard the expression before. She pretended to look almost *delighted* by such an insane non sequitur.

Mark said, "Does he believe in the sanctity of life?"

"Well, I'll tell you," her head began bobbling, addressing a larger audience that seemed to spread out behind him, "He does believe that Nod's life, if he'd lived, would have been about the same as ours. As yours and mine. Or anybody's. In terms of absolute value."

Absolute value. So there it was. She'd found a little friend to play a part in her melodrama with her, but a friend with a doctrine. Mark would be up against that form of bigotry. A "believer" steps inside the little transparent globe—the globe of his belief—and sees all things through it. The figure of Mark himself, seen through that globe, would condense into a selfish, evil man.

Because clearly, the kinds of people who "lead lives in delusion" are the ones who kill babies when they're defective because *they* want to be the Big American Winners. This was the new Lotta. She was branching out into the world. A child knows intimately where to hurt. Having been spoiled to perfection, a child naturally must turn around and inflict actual damage. The experiment in maturity isn't real if you don't inflict some real hurt. If the hurt is still only make-believe, then the long enchantment of childhood can't be broken; the princess stays forever sugar-frosted in her tower. She never begins the new work of whittling her parents back, pressing them back, toward their irrelevancy, irrelevancy being parents' perfection. Bodie, Bodie from Ohio, can't be entirely blamed for this. He just happened to come along. And he happened to come along just when she was starting to bring up private-school websites in her bedroom with the door closed.

Anyway this disclosure, in fact, explained a lot, now. It explained a certain quiet insubordination he'd felt moving beneath the surface of this whole Fantasy Weekend—like Bodie's seeming to smirk so confidently asking about the views of an "astrophysicist"—and Lotta's thrusting the *f*-word in his face—and at this point, the prospect of conversing with Bodie Lostig in a jail cell only made him tired, the truly dreary prospect, of having to do battle, sooner or later, with those innocent certainties.

A buzz penetrated the thick plate glass, the buzz of an outer door's lock being released. It was him.

THEY WATCHED THE anteroom through the shatterproof window. A policeman entered first and held the door, then the chair rolled in. The handsome, full-grown exemplary specimen, his cuffed hands in his lap, was being glided along by Officer McCuddy himself. The boy might have been inspecting his new hotel suite, looking around. Mark was a little ashamed of himself because he knew he was being unfair. A crippled young man is going to devise plenty of peculiar strategies for social success. Let him be a moral bully.

And *he* didn't really start this; Lotta started it, weeks ago. It was weeks ago that she began saying she would have been willing to sacrifice her education to stay home and care for the baby. And do the spoon-feeding. And if the swallow reflex didn't work, change his tubes twice a day. And put in the eyedrops if there were no blink reflex, and change the diapers, or the catheter too, depending. The little doomed effigy in the house, its ten years' trance of boredom, would have blotted out the ten years of *her* life from sixteen to twenty-six: those are important years. She claimed she wanted to read aloud to it, with the idea that something might be getting through. And play music, and rain forest sounds. So she claimed. Forgetting that when the chips were down, she was the first to advocate terminating it, sitting at the kitchen table. There was a great deal Mark might remind her of, tactfully, on the topic of her little inconsistencies.

They'd stood up to see, while Bodie's handcuffs were being removed and he was offered a wire basket. He gripped his own thigh to haul one leg up, and hooked an ankle on his knee and began untying his shoe. This particular chair's wheels were designed to slope inward, so it had a sporty look, as if it could take sharp corners at top speeds. For the occasion of their adventure tonight, he'd replaced the removable armrests. Even here in subjection, the boy naturally took an executive attitude that made these cops his servants accepting his shoes and bow tie. Lotta, beside Mark, radiated an adulation and an anxiety that were palpable. She almost rose on tiptoe in her yellow footies, watching him.

What made Lotta's whole melodrama unassailable was that, if you came out and *said* the little fetus was yet not a human life, you'd be shattering *her* fragile self-esteem: you'd be popping her bubble, and she somehow *was* the bubble, at the moment. The Celebrity Vacations environment only made it worse. By instant rumor, everybody on the trip knew why all the others were here—Rachel because her parents were divorcing, Danny Banzinetti because his father had moved out, Chang to cure his stutter. And Carlotta Perdue because HER LITTLE BROTHER DIED IN UTERO: that was the banner over her. That was the melodrama. There's no way to fight the melodrama; it's so widespread it can't be grabbed anywhere. Everybody knows it's fictive, but everybody goes along with it.

The guard with the black T-shirt approached the door of Large Meeting with his key. Now would come the ordeal of waiting together, the three of them in a bare room. With so much unsaid.

But the guard, when the door was open, told him, "Come with me, sir. The young lady stays here."

They would be separated, and Mark unreasonably panicked. "I'm her father. She's my daughter."

"Come with me, sir."

"I think they're just putting us in cells, Dad. It's okay."

"Couldn't we all be together?" he appealed to the guard, while yet obeying and following.

"Two males to holding in sally pod," the guard spoke to the walkie-talkie on his belt, pressing a thumb down on its button.

In response, the walkie-talkie gave him only a staticky burp, while he crossed the room with his one key—it was the master key apparently, for every door in the whole place—to take them out through another door, deeper into the institution. He had noticed that the floor out there was cement, not linoleum.

Separating him from Lotta, the door to Large Meeting was closed, with the 120-volt clank of its inner electromagnets.

His daughter, isolated now behind the plate glass, gave them both a wilting, consoling smile.

Bodie said, buoyantly, "Hey there, Mr. Perdue. How are ya?"

Officer McCuddy was already gone. Out the door. It might have been nice of him to say hi, at least. Meanwhile Mark's partner in crime, Bodie, was dismantling his tuxedo accessories to hand them over. Mark himself had never worn a tuxedo, but he had observed that they come with a lot of paraphernalia—shirt studs, clip-on things, cuff links—which now his wheelchair friend, one by one, removed and dribbled into the cellophane sandwich bag they held out for him, the same kind they'd given Mark for his pocket change. Now, for the duration of their time together in the slammer, Bodie's shirt panels would hang open unfastened, because the shirt had no buttons but only detachable studs. He apparently sunbathed, or went to a tanning salon, because his chest was caramel and smooth.

The prospect of having a word with Officer McCuddy was gone, and Mark found his feelings were actually a little hurt. He'd gone without offering so much as a greeting or a little backward salute, and Mark felt slighted; childishly, he felt deserted in the system. He'd thought they had a relationship, he and McCuddy—they'd chatted for a long time below the Hollywood Sign, out under the great radio-active smoothie of the Los Angeles night sky. They'd chatted about the ridiculous Celebrity Vacation business. And about McCuddy's own two sons. It had been generous of him, to depart from the usual arrest-procedure formality and (because they had to wait for the special wheelchair-accessible van) to kill time making conversation with a visiting tourist dad whose daughter was in a little trouble. McCuddy's sons were named Dion and Tedrow, they were sixteen and eleven, living in Anaheim with their mother. McCuddy admitted that both boys, at their separate ages, would benefit by an experience like this "fantasy vacation" thing, but when Mark coaxed his real opinions out of him, McCuddy confessed with a twinkle, that, yes, at bottom the celebrity vacation was bullshit. It was Mark who introduced that word. McCuddy folded his hands before his belt buckle and looked up at the night sky and agreed, gently, ruefully, "The very soul of bullshit," in almost a gospel singer's warble. He'd thought they were friends. Usually cops are constrained to being tight-lipped. You never get a cop who can be informal. But now that he was behind bars—or behind shatterproof plate glass—he was as invisible to McCuddy as all the other souls who had passed in among these walls. McCuddy's interest now was in getting back in his patrol car, going out again into the vast Los Angeles night, and seeing what else might be going wrong, where he could intervene. He might have at least nodded, or flipped a hand.

He and Bodie were being led along a broad corridor inside the building. "So, how've they been treating us, Mr. Perdue?" said Bodie. "Learn anything?" He was speaking over his shoulder, seated and rolling, as Mark, under the hand of his own escort, was following the guard-propelled chair. They were deep in the jailhouse, passing heavy-looking doors as they went along, each with a little vertical window-pane. The whole place looked deserted. No criminals tonight, for the beautiful new wing of the Santa Monica jail, built-to-code and wheel-chair-accessible. The floor in this deeper dungeon wasn't linoleum any-more, it was concrete, burnished a glossy bronze by a process favored among interior decorators of the past decade. Indeed, it was the exact same curing-staining-sealing-buffing treatment as the floor at that bar the Studio Lot. All the lights in the place seemed motion-activated, and a fleet of overhead fluorescents came stuttering and storming to life, at an L in the corridor, where they swung into another receiving area. This one was larger—there was a long baby-blue Formica coun-ter—and *four* computers, all just as pristine in their disuse as the one in the front receiving area. In this area, jailers could check in criminals in batches. Four at a time.

Bodie (since Mark hadn't responded) asked the question again, "Did you learn, for instance, if there's a fine?" He wrenched his torso around in his wheelchair. "You know, Mr. Perdue, I'm going to want to pay the fine. This is all my fault. I'm the one who had to touch the Hollywood Sign."

The one guard spoke into his communication device, "Two males, one disabled, in the number three sally cell."

Here, now, was the more standard form of jailhouse accommodation: vertical metal bars, painted the old Wrigley's Doublemint green. A bed in the shape of a raised platform of solid cement. A toilet that lacked a hinged seat, so it was just a stainless steel cylinder.

Which he hoped Bodie wouldn't need to use. Nor he himself need to use.

With a TV-crime-drama clang of the gate, they were locked in together, unceremoniously, without any instructions to stay in view of the camera in the upper corner. Mark knew, if he asked the guards about their situation, what the answer would be: that right now their paperwork was being done; nothing could happen until their paperwork was done. They walked off making no explanation or farewell, side by side, talking on some topic apparently far from their jailhouse job.

So Mark sat down on the cement, sarcophagus-sized platform. Which had no mattress or pad. Bodie would have his wheelchair.

As far as topics of conversation went, they didn't have much in common. Yet they also, certainly, had plenty to talk about. Somewhere inside the suave boy was the utopian who was turning his daughter into "a humbler person," as well as helping her feel guilty about her little brother. Mark had an idea that if he just listened and gave the boy enough rope, enough character defects would become clear. At least one true deal killer. Because Lotta was smart. By the end of the weekend he might have gathered some "evidence against" him, or anyway at least somehow gotten to the bottom of this person.

"I REGRET TO OBSERVE," he said, and he added the name, "*Bodie*," somewhat genially, as they settled in, "that it's beginning to look like this will endanger your plans to go walking on the beach tomorrow."

"Ah." He made a socked-in-the-jaw gesture of assent. "The way things are going, yes." He was wheeling his chair to a better position in the cell. It was like backing a cannon into position. Then he offered, "I'll explain that to you, if you like. Why Lotta and I felt we don't need to do the rest of the Celebrity events." He did his trick of growing taller in the chair. "For one thing we're just *older* than that, Lotta and I. Don't get me wrong, the Celebrity Vacation people do an excellent job. They're great," and he quoted the promotional material, "They '*Make Make-Believe Seem Real!*' But—" he shrugged all around, at the condition of being older now. At least too old for make-believe.

Mark was scanning the limits of their new home, but peripherally he was taking in the figure before him. The long wavy golden hair; the square jaw; in the open shirt panels the muscular chest, smooth and hard as taffy; the powerful shoulders—all dwindling below into his occult half, his "feminine half," as Mark found he thought of it, because the boy had a habit of, as if demurely, twisting in his chair to sit high on one hip, then high on the other, training his thighs always

171

together. Back home in Ohio, he was president of the senior class and his grade point average was *above* 4.0, which according to Lotta is a feat you can accomplish by taking Advanced Placement classes. Also, he had a rock band, back there in Shaker Heights. He convened them for rehearsals in his own basement every weekend, whipping them along from his drum throne.

"I'm sure a 'Fantasy Vacation' is good for some people," he went on. Bodie was like the other boy, the one from Winnetka; they both had this precocious way of talking. Inside his little bubble of rhetoric, he probably felt quite lubricated and easy, unthinking that, to an adult, outside the bubble observing, the quaintness was alarming and swollen. "I think the Fantasy Vacation thing was good for me last year when I did it. It came along at a certain *point* in my life." But that point in his life was long past, and he opened his hands, to display himself now, how well he'd turned out. "Also, I think it's good for people like Josh and Rachel, who have real talent and real *plans* to *be* performers. They're amazing. And David too. And it's good for someone like Danny Banzinetti who's at a stage of *his* psychosexual development. He might benefit by something like this."

Hearing a boy at this age use the expression *psychosexual*, Mark had to glance to Bodie's face, golden-tanned, beetling with sincerity. "But your daughter," his expression grew tender, "We've had some amazing conversations. She's so great. And we just *decided*. We just *said* this is ridiculous. We said, let's be real. It's ridiculous. Look at it. When you're putting a lot of effort into making yourself a 'Celebrity,' and you see the state of the world?"

"Well, Bodie. Let me just say that I don't disapprove out of hand. Not of walks on the beach. Not at all. I assume that such decisions as you and Lotta make are esoteric to yourselves, and you have every right to use this time as you see fit." (Why was he talking in this stilted way?) "If you want to walk on the beach, I think that could be a fine way of using this time, which, after all, was always devised for your indulgence. It's your vacation, this weekend."

He had to wonder whether Lotta had mentioned to him her little insight—that Dad and the escort seemed to be sweet on each other. Knowing Lotta, she would keep surmises to herself. But if she *had* mentioned it, Bodie might perceive a secret motive in a father's permissive lenience now. For, when the grown-up chaperones don't have to spend the last day of the trip watching one more taping or one more rehearsal, then *they*—Mark and Blythe—have the day off to themselves.

"You know something? Dr. Perdue?" With a twist of a big wheel, he wedged forward. "I'm serious when I say this. I've always wanted to talk to an astrophysicist. Now that we're stuck in here for a little while, can I ask a couple of 'dumb'-type questions? Things I've always wondered?"

Mounted on his mobile stupa, his pedestal on wheels, Bodie Lostig was in fact a kind of centaur, wily and strong. In the role of suitor he apparently wanted to actually grapple about this here. Mark, in his unreadiness, began evasively by yielding ground: "Bodie, you know, a scientist becomes so specialized, you'd be amazed sometimes, how ignorant a scientist is of the whole general field. People just tend to know their one little thing."

"I'm really just asking the old What-Are-Things-Made-Of question. I mean really. I mean *below* atoms and quarks and superstrings. When you get down to it."

Mark smiled. "Nobody knows, of course." He smiled harder.

Bodie just kept staring.

"The main thing about being a scientist, Bodie, is what you *don't* know. That's you're guiding light: your ignorance. I can't describe this, but it gets to be a funny mental habit. What you think you *do* know— 'Knowledge'—isn't interesting anymore after a while. You actually dismiss things, or rather ignore things, and don't have it all wrapped up neatly in your mind. So-called knowledge is possibly harmful, to deeper understanding. So really you delve in *your* little place and stop paying much attention to a lot of the 'certainties' and 'verities' and things long-settled. Nothing is much settled, ideally."

He had talked about his job this way before, plenty of times; so did everybody; it was, in the profession, a standard song and dance; but at this moment, he really did see his own workaday fuzzy indeterminacy as forlorn, or else heroic; same thing. Maybe it was because he was trying to explain it to a religious fundamentalist, sitting smiling his unconvinced smile. Or it was that he was viewing his own ordinary life now from an actual "jail cell," for an hour seated upon the public cement pew of consideration and remorse. Every day in Berkeley's corridors he was a ghost, a bewildered, confused ghost, that rare tingle of apparent consciousness in the universe, arriving at his office doorway and tapping his office key on his own upper lip, lower lip, left cheek, and right cheek, then touching the key to the door above and below the knob and to left and right of the knob, before inserting it. "It's a habit of mind. You kind of get dumber as you go in deeper. That is, if you're in research. Not everybody is in research."

Bodie kept gazing.

"The short answer to your question, right at the moment, is 'strings.' They're the new version of 'particle.' Now strings are the smallest." (From his expression, Bodie had already heard all about strings.) "Take the nucleus of an atom. Strings are twenty billion

billion times smaller than that. That's small. Twenty billion billion is a lot. I don't know if you can picture that. You know how many a billion is. Well, multiply a billion of those billions. That's the factor. The factor smaller than an atom's nucleus. Which was, already, pretty small."

"All right, but then, what are strings made of?"

"Made of? Strings are our own pictures. They are our own cartoons. Strings are some kind of entities which vibrate '*like*' the musical tones of tiny strings. So they have that quality. Of mathematically vibrating. The picture fits mathematical models."

"And I'm saying what are they *made of*? What's vibrating? There's some little *thing* vibrating."

"Oh," Mark with happiness saw what a pure question he was asking, and he would dispose of it with relish. "Now you're asking a theological question."

Bodie let his eye drift aside while his brain was going clickety-clack. "No," he came back. "Everything is made of something. Some kind of stuff. That's science, that's not theology."

"The idea of 'stuff' is religion. A physicist knows things are only made of information. They're made of our observations. There's no basic 'clay.' Except in the Bible. That's where we got misled: the Bible: in Genesis: that clay."

Bodie stared at him while his mind made an effort to knit around this. Things, mystically, are made of our seeing them. If the young man *was* a believer, he might regard such a point of view as nihilism and despair. Or even deviltry. Baha'i religion was a complete blank spot. But one does have the impression most religions tend to feel threatened: religion is the war against death, and it's futile; it's the hope for something supernatural. (In Mark's own mind, honestly, his only belief was that the world *is* supernatural, but that's never quite relevant.)

He went on, "In the Bible, 'clay' was the basic stuff. Before God got to it, the clay was just sitting there and it was dead and stupid, supposedly. So people still view particles that way. Inert like clay. And *free of information* like clay. In fact, you know, in truth, the photons zipping around this room right now," he dipped his hand upward into the bath of light particles from the fluorescents, "are immortal. Time actually *does not pass*, for little light particles zipping around. That form of eternity is all around us." He was just trying to amaze and affright the boy now, and awe him.

Looking up at the lights, Bodie said, "Whew. That's hard to picture."

It was the response—the concession of wonder—Mark supposed he'd aimed at.

But then the rolling bust of a sphinx that was Bodie Lostig folded his powerful forearms over his chest, and he scowled, coming up with something. He was one of those people whose hands seldom or never come near his face. Mark habitually observed this distinction in people: a certain kind of person—a kind who seems at a special or even unfair advantage in life—never touches his face or nose or mouth, whereas his daughter Lotta was an instance of one who is constantly rubbing and scratching and smudging the clarity of her pretty features. The attraction of this boy, for Lotta, would be his statuary upper half—the lower half sunken, submerged, wavery—so when the two kids kissed and fondled in the back seat of their limo, he had to suppose, Lotta would have been in love with an iconic "handsomeness," which, however, was planted in a nether world, of passive vulnerability. She would have played the part of flame around him, in her own mind. It seemed the only way to imagine the necessary eroticism.

Bodie, behind his folded forearms, had hit on a way to disagree, frowning. "'Time' would still be passing, though. Maybe the photon hasn't *changed* since it was created. *Not changing* can seem like timelessness. But time is still going on. Time is," his hands tossed air, ". . . *time.*"

"No, this is old, settled Einstein. Little tiny subatomic fast things are literally outside time. We, us, we're *inside* time. We're big, slow creatures, so we experience time." He lifted his arms, like a sleepwalker's arms, showing himself as an example: large, complicated, bewildered creature, doomed, hulking, silhouetted in eternity's spangled shimmer. "You know, we humans are incredibly slow compared to the speed of the universe. Compared to the speed of the big bang. Which we're in the middle of. The universe is happening really fast, instantly fast. It *seems* like forever to *us.*" (Bodie looked dully uncomprehending.) "What time is, is, time seems to be an 'emergent' phenomenon in the universe. That's the word they use. Time emerged. It came out of other more fundamental things, like mass and space. During a tiny period they call the Planck era. Whether there was time *before*: that's a debate. Time probably didn't emerge till later."

"'Later' after . . . ?"

"After whatever the big bang was."

"Yeah, right. When, supposedly, there was 'nothing.'"

The boy—could it be?—seemed to jeer at the notion of a big bang.

If Bodie Lostig *were* a bona fide fundamentalist—the complete package!—then Mark would despair but also he'd rejoice, because then he'd have his deal killer. Lotta, too, will see it.

Bodie said in dismay, "There would still be 'time,' even when there's nothing. Even if there's nothingness everywhere. Still, *time* would be there. Ticking away. Only without clocks or anything."

Shamelessly in his effort to goad the person inside there, Mark kept doubling back, "Well, there does seem to be such a thing as total nothingness." He positively leered.

"Ah. Like nothingness between atoms," Bodie said. It was something he would have heard in high school.

"Actually, between atoms, no, it isn't a vacuum. It's packed with energy and stuff, and potential mass. But there may once have been true 'nothingness,' back at one point, back outside the quantum event people call the big bang."

Bodie waited for more info, his clear Baha'i gaze scanning for error. His Adult Children of Alcoholics gaze.

"I phoned our driver, by the way," Mark said. "She's going to find some money for us, for bail. She ought to be here soon. Did anybody phone your parents back home?"

"There's no such thing as totally nothing," Bodie's hands lay together in his lap, palms up. "Because imagine this." He closed his eyes and spoke: "Imagine some kind of place that's empty, empty in all directions forever—if that's what nothingness is—imagine that situation. Well *still*, even in *that* situation, two plus two would still equal four." He opened his eyes. "And all the other laws: multiplication and division. And calculus, too. Algebra. All of it would be there already. Maybe you'll say 'time' doesn't pass in the vacuum, but still, in that empty place, two plus two would equal four. The *math* is there. It's always everywhere. The *law* would still be hanging out there, in the vacuum."

His lids had sprung open and his gaze was so intense, so imploring, the eyes actually pressed closer together, squeezing the little spongiform organ that was Bodie's soul. "Wouldn't it? Still equal four? Even in a vacuum?"

"Interesting!" Mark groaned, revolving away on his cement seat.

At last his own accumulated tiredness had arrived. It combined with the force of Bodie's little intellectual challenge, forming a wave he couldn't breast. Weariness made him rise up—and stand up—from the cold cement pad that was supposed to be a cot and go have a peek out through the cage wall. He gripped the vertical bars, like a typical jailbird. Still, nothing was out there but the four never-used computers along a solid Formica counter. Nothing in sight. Not even a Bic pen. Because of course a Bic pen could serve as a weapon: some crazy inmate could grab it and stab somebody. A jail *is* a place where the flow of "time" comes to a halt. Little box of eternity. His cellmate Bodie Lostig was the kind of kid he'd shied away from in high school, enthusiastic, diligent high-achievers broadcasting a personal inner radiance that cancels all shadows around themselves, people for whom everything seems simple, so therefore it all does come up simple. Everything *is* simple in the vicinity of such people. Which is why you have to get away from them. He wondered if, for Lotta, that was the appeal. Simplicity. Answers. He hoped not.

"You know, Bodie, Lotta tells me—or she kind of implies—that there's a kind of whole *moral* aspect. Dropping out of all the Celebrity festivities. A kind of ethical, moral, *moralistic* aspect to that." He did feel himself a sneaky bully luring the boy out into the open. He got more specific: "All the gasoline and jet fuel it takes to fly out. The ecological mess of it all. So Lotta says."

Bodie was looking at him, but he seemed to be seeing something else, something very different from Mark, which he was considering in a new light. At last he said with a soothing empathy, "You know, Mr. Perdue, *I'm* scientific. I know we're evolved from little chemicals in the sea. And from . . ." he plapped his two hands on the armrests, "stardust. I know we're machines, biological machines. And our 'minds' are only just electrical impulses. And hormones. Our thoughts, our idealistic 'ideas': just hormones and enzymes and excuses. Just electrochemical blips running around the brain. We're machines, survival machines, you and I." Like an invitation to fight, his one hand beckoned, rollingly, in the space between them. "Aren't we. Evolved from DNA. Just for survival reasons."

This was slightly alarming; it was a sort of taunt, or a sort of upbraiding, and Mark actually shrank back a little, because this was a small room with just the two of them. In a way, he was pleased, because now the young man had shown himself, and if he was capable of a kind of bizarre irrelevant ranting, he might be ruled out of Lotta's life with good reason. Bodie went on in the same theme, gripping a good pinch of his own dead thigh meat illustratively, "So we're like Frankenstein machines, I know. Making little *noises* at each other, on this planet. Just *noises* we've evolved socially. Noises that are intelligible to each other. And they're socially . . . socially 'useful,'" he condoled. "But we're basically selfish. *Pretending* we've got high intentions and, like, 'motives' and 'altruism.' 'Cause that's a social thing, too: 'altruism.' We all have to seem altruistic. But really, all we're *programmed* to do is survive. Take advantage of each other and exploit each other. Really we just want to defeat each other in natural selection. As robots, biologically." He gave one more shake to the thigh in his grip, his attached other half. "Robots. From atoms on up. So, I do see all that."

He seemed to have made his point then, and his hand pressed out in the direction of Mark's knee, as if to apply the balm of commiseration. He smiled. End of sermon.

So Mark was starting to see satisfaction, maybe. Because now at last this was the famous other side of Bodie, a side where the word *crazy* might apply, or at least the word *inappropriate*. *That Bodie, he's pretty intense*, Rachel in the little bar had said. Now in watching a bright, sociopathic young person trot out his little performance, he could only wonder where he'd gotten it from. From what Baha'i youth discussion group did this line of moral philosophy originate, sarcasm and all?

More likely, it came from the meetings in church basements with children of alcoholics, where on weeknights God manifests Himself like a tacked-up instructional visual aid. Those kinds of get-togethers have tables of free "literature" and brochures, and you get your little handbook with placemark ribbons. Gilt-edge pages. Daily prayers and affirmations, doctrines and maxims, rules to live by. All to help the birth-defective boy start grooming himself as the designated family Hero. In a family-structure where "the father" was the designated Problem. So the Ohio boy in Mark's view was starting to develop a few details in his life story, and Mark had to admit, he found him slightly brave, to be brandishing these toy swords of his in Mark's face, in this situation in a jail cell together.

"Anyway, yes, there's the environmental issue with this expensive trip," Bodie swung back, quite calmly, as if he hadn't just made a huge illogical swerve in the direction of preaching. As if that completely irrelevant little *paragraph* of his had been delivered by some stand-in actor, who was now gone.

"There's the jet fuel all right. Not to mention—oh, you name it— laundering linens in the hotel, burning gasoline so *we* can go cruising around in stretch limousines drinking corn-based artificial sweeteners. All that." He smiled. That smile, it was always like a rinsing facial splash. "But also, mainly, Lotta and I just wanted to just walk on the beach. It started to seem like a waste of our last day together, not seeing each other."

He was starting to appear as a harmless, containable threat, a boy who sits around saying *Whenever we turn on a lightbulb something dies out there*, and Mark began to realize he'd been hosting that heart attack feeling, which he really might shrug off, and burst through, with a deeper breath. For a minute there, it was scary, when from his wheelchair he'd beckoned, saying we're all cold-blooded monsters. One couldn't help but think he was talking about himself: that his own admitted motive was to reproduce with the daughter.

But at some point right back there—right at the point of corn-based artificial sweeteners!—he started to deflate back to the normal size of a seventeen-year-old. If this whole situation had been feeling as if they were two wizards from opposed cults hurling their bolts at each other, then Mark Perdue would definitely be the old, dark one, Bodie the untested boy-wizard, and right now all the boy-wizard's spells had curdled on his hands.

A distant door in the building made a clang. Maybe at last, this wing of the jail would start to get a few proper criminals. Mark, his back against the bars, was a shell open to the empty exterior. In the depths of the jailhouse corridor—somewhere around the L-shaped corner—two guards could be heard talking, chuckling about something, headed the other way, voices dwindling. It was a female voice and a male voice, both with a bored, easy familiarity, government employees fated to work side by side for years. And get along. Until retirement or until job transfer. All that was in their voice tones, all that resignation in their life trajectories, all their second-bestness, their bluffing.

It was a comfort to hear them out there, just in case his zealot cellmate might, yes, conceivably become even more inappropriate somehow. Blythe, by this time, might be out in the front offices somewhere, with her envelope of hundred-dollar bills, trying to get the attention of whomever was in charge. But in places like this nobody was in charge, especially after midnight, every officeholder on the shift was just a passenger within the system, getting through the night, lodged deep in the belly of the beast. By daylight, too, *non*responsibility *and* *non*responsiveness are the bureaucrat's code. The bureaucrat's rule is, do as little as possible. Be blameworthy for nothing. Soon (or at least inevitably, before they could be released) one of those guards would come around with papers to be signed, papers no guard had ever really looked at, papers nobody had bothered to focus on, not ever, during all the years of working here, all legal boilerplate, pages specifying the prisoner's personal effects that had been surrendered to storage baskets, pages indemnifying the city and county of Los Angeles, etc., pages defining the terms of arrest, the terms of release, the rights of the accused. Et cetera. Those four computers did look never-used. Jail is limbo.

Bodie's sermon, he decided—of course—was aimed to condemn the abortion of Noddy. That was the point. That was its mysterious relevance, the reason for the gleam in his eye as he spoke. Describing a world populated by biological machine-monsters, he'd been mocking "materialism." In his little system, Mark and Audrey Perdue had terminated their baby because they saw the boy's death as practical, utilitarian, and convenient. What else could the sermon's relevance be? Mark and Audrey had killed the fetus because it would have been competing with them for resources. The resources were: house, 3BR 2BA with walk-in closet, cars in carport, the freedom to work productively in society and have that dignity, leisure time to watch television, open weekends.

Which, in a sense, was true. Strange to admit. As a kind of oversimplification it was partly accurate, yes, but innocent, and innocence is ruthless.

"Any-hoo . . . yes, Mr. Perdue," said Bodie. "Lotta and I do have reasons, for skipping the rest of the expensive Celebrity activities.

Environmentally, the world's getting smaller. We're using up the planet and having no conscience. I guess, if Lotta's been mentioning all that, I probably sound like a fanatic. I *am* a fanatic."

A disabled person, he'd noticed, has the ability to exploit the small motions of the chair as a form of self-assertion, it's like a bodily extension, backing off a few ticks or inching forward, or reangling the position by a couple of degrees, expressively, convivially. Bodie had a talent for sometimes casually *flipping* the chair back into a wheelie and sustaining that balance aslant in comfort, without a hint of a uni-cyclist's wobble. This seemed definitely *not* one of the moments for doing a wheelie, here in a jail cell, facing the father of the girl he'd kissed. Rather he sat up straight, in the asana of one interviewing for a job, hands in lap.

"I understand you've started an organization back in Ohio, there, Bodie." (He was not proud of himself, seeing himself repeatedly hold-ing out new hoops for the boy to jump through.) "An organization where each individual's front yard will be—you know—vegetable gar-den, hog, clothesline . . ."

Bodie's only response was to wave the topic off, smiling. "It wouldn't interest you, Mr. Perdue. It's just a lot of 'make-a-better-future' stuff."

Making a better future was evidently not for Mark and his generation.

"Lotta tells me you have a far-reaching notion of 'crimes against humanity': people should produce what they need, don't exploit any-body else, don't use up the natural resources, don't even *buy* anything! Kind of do away with the whole economy! Well, I actually don't see anything particularly wrong with that—I really don't—I think it's great—but when you say 'crime against humanity,' sometimes aren't you just talking about *moms* who are just trying to drive their kids to school? So they need to burn a little gasoline?"

Bodie didn't answer but only smiled mildly—and expectantly, too—a guru, waiting for Mark to hear and detect his own errors, making of himself "a still pool" to mirror Mark's image.

Mark added, "Maybe the gasoline comes from some underdeveloped little *place*, but nevertheless—"

Bodie began, "You know, I'd like to try just planting a seed," his hands were making a shy cup, drifting out from his lap. "Let me just try planting this one little seed. Which might sprout at some later date. Something for you to think about. You know in the South . . ." Here he went again. Mark with relish drew back into his observatory pit. Bodie Lostig was so conceited he was positively luminous. "In the South in 1840-whatever, there were people who quietly just freed their slaves. Way before the Civil War. At that time, most people—good abolitionist people, too!—were saying it was still unrealistic to try freeing the slaves. Or, like one might say, not just idealistic but actually impractical. They weren't racist at all. Their point was, society wasn't ready yet. Or the slaves would feel displaced, and they'd be exploited in the job market, and would be operating at a huge, huge disadvantage. And end up in ghettos. All crime-ridden. Or the freed slaves will just be enslaved all over again, in the industrial factory system. Or, that that whole farm-labor system was still necessary for efficient business practice and would have to end *gradually*. Nobody felt 'evil,' they just felt like they had to compromise realistically with reality, and how things were presently working. But still, a few people did free their slaves and *took* the business loss. They *ate* that loss. And probably looked a little weird, or a little stupid. They just quietly *did* it. Slaves were huge investments, you know, for the average farmer. It's like, nowadays, a farmer investing in a big tractor or combine-thing. Slaves cost a lot! Average little farmers, back then, they couldn't afford to be idealistic, if they had one or two slaves. Like how, today, people drive cars and never think about it. People don't worry about it. They just hop in the car and go. They don't feel like *they're* genocidal when they drive around."

Bodie pushed his tuxedo sleeves back to the elbows, demonstrating there was no trickery, and he showed both his open hands. "The ideal society someday, Mr. Perdue, would be *post*economic. We would live like the American Indians used to. Or like the places we bomb—you know—the conservative little villages? With oxcarts and women-all-in-black? We would ideally start living like them. We need to bomb them, presently these days, so we can have air-conditioning. And one day get *them* air-conditioning. That's also why we're killing the oceans and everything else: so we can get *everybody* air-conditioning, even the people we bomb. Nowadays people look back at slavery, or Nazi Germany, and they say, 'How could those people be so awful, back then? How could those people be so evil?' They say, 'If *I'd* lived back in the South, I would have freed *my* slaves. And *I* would have helped a family of Jews. I would have been one of the good people.'" His hands rose and patted down the seed he'd planted. "Just something I thought you might like to think about."

The smile: it was the gentle smile of the transcendent. He seemed always to be holding in reserve a more difficult opinion, mercifully, tactfully. It was impossible to define the exact superior niche he pretended to speak from. But he was a nightmare bulging forward, pontifical, a hand puppet despite the gap of air between his platform and the floor, a jack-in-the-box that from its lidded casket lunges and sways and swings. This was the fruit that was saved from the abortionist's knife, exemplary in righteousness, self-equipped with ideals that will give it a reason for thriving.

"After total environmental collapse, people will look back at us. When people of the future look back at what *we* killed, it wasn't Jews or African Americans, or one race or another. It was actually bigger than that, what we killed. We're doing something actually bigger than genocide." He gestured at Mark, because Mark was an instance. "Every day, bigger than genocide."

The surrounding angry dimness was mostly from not having slept or eaten. Surely all the boy was doing, in his own mind, was delivering a speech like a student working for an A in public speaking.

"It's everything we are," he went on, patting his own upper body, from his pectorals to his abs. His dead legs didn't get the thumping, because they were the part of him that had already been fed forward into oblivion. "Everything we are, and everything we do, is basically ruining everything."

He was going to be interrupted, because the original two guards were coming around the L-corner. One of them spoke to his belt-mounted radio, "Two males to release."

The other was digging in his belt to bring up the single big key that opened every door. He and the wheelchair kid would be free, Blythe would be waiting outside, and the little jail-cell encounter was over. Just in time. He'd started to feel surges.

But he had evidence now. The boy had shown himself to be, if not exactly crazy, at least insolent. At least inappropriate. With a little time away, Mark would be able to get him in perspective. He was only a seventeen-year-old. And he was physically disabled. Which, along with his dysfunctional home life, had made him permanently angry at the world—and he had discovered one refrain, which it pleased him to keep harping on: his own righteousness: it was like a bagpipe he'd discovered and kept reinflating to make it drone in people's faces. Also, nobody liked him. None of the other kids. They all made fun of him. Lotta was too smart for this. Mark tried to command the boy, by force of telepathy, to stop lecturing now, because the two guards would find him apparently receiving spiritual advice from a seventeen-year-old.

The one guard said, "Time to go, gentlemen," inserting his key.

As now there wasn't much time, Bodie shrank his message to a pill: "A person's happiness isn't going to come from anything you *get* for *yourself*, like 'prosperity' or success or whatever."—Or like freedom from a brain-damaged baby. He made the shrug-smirk.

The guard swung open the gate to free them, saying, for the other guard's amusement, with a weary scoop of the eyes, "Yeah, right this way, Mahatma."

ALONG THE CEMENT corridor, behind the guard pushing the wheelchair, Mark followed his uniformed, jingling, radio-crackling captors—on out to freedom—but he wasn't seeing anything because he'd begun to feel dizzy in that cell. Listening to the moral lesson and looking at the jack-in-the-box, he'd started getting the swarming sensation in the throat, the emergency hopelessness. An average human being is complicated and has no real defenses ordinarily. Against the attack of the simplistic. Bodie, while making his eye twinkle, had spoken of casual, everyday genocide, which was a code word. The lesson was, the Perdue family should have given over ten years of their lives to the infant in its twilight. That's what glinted in Bodie's eye. He couldn't say it, not in an explicit way. The baby ought to be suffering at home in a crib in the spare bedroom where ordinarily the bikes are stored and the never-used glossy Weber barbecue with the price tags still hanging on it. Under the terms of society's conversation, nobody is allowed to speak honestly, or even allowed to think honestly—society simply places people in roles in a formal melodrama, so the melodrama replaces thinking. Lotta and her new boyfriend were pretending something mattered, where, really, they didn't care. The boy didn't care. Nobody cared. The melodrama consists in people's *pretending* passionately to care. And it causes in others a hopelessness, and a weakness, and the sense of a smothering wall. Mark ought to take care of his health and get back to the hotel room and lie down and maybe get a snack in his stomach.

Then there was Blythe. When the heavy door was buzzed open, he caught sight of her, the chipmunk profile, separated by one last barrier of glass. She was standing at a counter, feeding paper money into the steel bowl under an armored window. She was his ally in the world, the mature world, the ripe, full, dappled world.

He didn't see his daughter, however, not anywhere. She wasn't visible through the big window in the room called Large Meeting.

Before he could ask where she was, Bodie asked first, looking up to the guards, from his parked seat, in his self-assured tone referring to her as "Carlotta."

Neither of the two jailers answered. They ignored him. So the Celebrity turned his attention away idly, idly to examine a few miscellaneous "Know Your Rights" notices on the wall. He was a boy who was angry about his own weakness and powerlessness. It would be a permanent, chronic kind of anger, a fundamental anger. And so as revenge he had found a way of belittling the world. Mark kept an analytic eye on him because such people are poisonous, because they do pretend to believe it. They pretend for *their own* spectatorship: they're watching themselves "believe" something; they think the pretense might bring about the real thing, true belief. They know in their deepest heart none of it's true. And call that faith. What they really like, though, is holding it up against others, like a candle.

At this point the boy had nothing more to say to Mark and seemed satisfied to disregard him. He had delivered his blow. It was a glancing, indirect blow, delivered diagonally through Mark's daughter, but it would go on spreading: the infant's stunted life ought to have been lived out to completion, in the crib with the IV bottle, the becalmed mobile motionless over him, unseen, where he would have heard only the few ambient sounds, like television or the vacuum cleaner or the dishwasher, or a distant lawn mower, which would represent the outer world, the mysterious sunny spaces beyond a window sill. Lotta had said it, *Bodie does believe Nod's life would have had the same absolute value,* the same as people who got the complete eighty years, like people who taught physics or defended corporations from lawsuits or built low-income housing *or whatever:* ten years of paralysis and incomprehension had the same "value," supposedly. Hearing a distant lawn mower once a week was supposed to have comparable worth. The orbit of the neighbor's lawn mower would have been, from within the boy's crib, an event as important as the northern lights. The touch of his sister's hand wiping the cold spit from his chest would have been, to him, all possible communion. The sound of the vacuum cleaner would have been Beethoven and Mozart. The clank of dishes in the sink, after dinner, would have been the Grand Canyon and the Milky Way. The jay's harsh song outside his window would have been as important as all poetry, everything in Wittgenstein and Shakespeare and Newton's *Principia.* All he and Audrey had to show, now, was leisure time and disposable income. That's what Bodie's kind of philosophy proposed; but the truth is, a physicist and a lawyer are worth more than a paralyzed, retarded, blind baby, that's an objective social fact you have to take responsibility for, because if you don't, then you do live in a world where the evening sound of dishes is as great as the Milky Way, or just the sensation of cotton fabric is as profound as the Seven Wonders of the World.

"WHERE *IS* THE wine list?" Blythe said, unzipping her jacket, opening the heavy padded spiral-bound book of snacks, cocktails, in-room movies, dessert offerings, masseuses, banquet rooms, spas and salons, boutiques and concierge services. "Have any preferences?"

During the drive back she'd used her cell phone to call ahead and order a room service cart to Mark's room, a midnight meal devised—part medicinal, part triumphal—for the returning hero: cold salmon with a French name, a fruit-and-cheese plate, a bread basket. She had put off ordering wine because she wanted to see the list. Mark did feel deserving. He felt altogether better, too. He'd withstood the ordeal of the disabled boy who was such a superior human being, he hadn't lost control and said anything to bring him down, so he'd survived with his dignity intact. Like one of those martyrs, he'd been penned with a beast and, surviving, he'd only been made stronger by it. After the drive back to the hotel—(Bodie riding royally in front, father and daughter crammed into the back seat together, the collapsed wheelchair behind them in the hatchback, crushing Blythe's NORTON SIMON MUSEUM gift shop bag, the painful kneeling before Bodie so that his passenger seat could be adjusted to make legroom)—then after all the accounts of how *boring!* a jailhouse is—and how amazingly *impolite!* jailers can be—after the kids' tireless excited boasting about the wonders of beachgoing wheelchairs—and after the two young Celebrities had been installed in their separate Celebrity Suites to sleep—it was still only two in the morning. And in the room the meal was already there, on a wheeled gurney under a linen shroud, and Mark was able to close his (hefty, armored, veneered) hotel room door on everything, with a brass *clack* in the latch, and he went straight for the bed and sat himself up against the pillows, with his jacket still on, and his shoes still on. Let Blythe use the armchair across the room. Let her bring him tidbits on plates. He carried on talking, unburdening himself of his many insights into the boy and his weird oratory. He didn't feel tired anymore. He'd never felt better. *Annoyance* had cheered him up, at least temporarily. And the boy's style of pronouncements, their free-floating grandeur, was so interesting. Also, he was excited because there was something fascinating now: he wanted to get back home and talk with Audrey: about this $2 + 2 = 4$ thing. Audrey was always his first listener.

And it was a problem. It was a problem that a boy from Cleveland—in his ignorance, not giving it a second thought—had lifted and dropped without realizing what he was saying. The so-called creation instant, the instant when mass and energy were first fossilized in the expansion—all that mass beading up from nothing—that moment was acknowledged all through the profession to be, still, a fiction; but before that instant, all of mathematics had already, always, waited. Mathematics seems not exactly a fiction, not in quite the same way as particles and energy are. Mathematics might have already been there in some sense.

And apparently nobody, so far, had found that reflection peculiar, or troubling, or amusing. Nobody right now in Karlsruhe. He had to wonder why *he* was troubled by it. In a few days, he might mention it to Audrey. See what she comes back with. He didn't yet want to look directly at it, himself. He knew from experience, the way to make a problem grow is simply to ignore it, exist alongside it, glance at it only sidelong from time to time, and avoid frightening it off. Maybe it would turn out to be nothing.

He even had a plan: to bring it up saying he'd run across it somewhere online in an abstract of someone else's article. Bringing it up as his own idea would make Audrey respond more guardedly, artificially, because of how she took care of him. He would even say he found the idea objectionable. That would be how to plant the idea. Audrey sooner or later would have a response. It was Audrey who, fifteen years ago, had set him off on a new idea by suggesting, innocently, that space implied time because "distance is always a matter of time, isn't it?" Her view of physics was always as pure as a fresh-bloomed lily, and he always watched closely, after having set a new notion within that cup. He knew her well, and he knew if he brought this up as his own new idea, her response wouldn't be honest or naive. He would bring it up during her glass of Guinness. *So I ran across something preposterous on abstracts.com today.*

"It is now the moment," Blythe whispered with her head bowed, "for a very deep red."

She was pondering the book of choices. Meanwhile she was shedding her jacket to reveal yet another wardrobe change of the evening. She must have stopped by home again. For a jailhouse visit, she'd outfitted herself in a tight knit shirt that was both turtlenecked and sleeveless, baring her shoulders while shackling her neck. But the same jeans as before.

"Throw me the remote, would you?" Mark said, because in fact he did want the TV screen flickering, on mute.

She tossed him the button-studded wand while she picked up the phone to order. What materialized on the screen was the hotel's continuous video loop, of well-made, paired beds, colorful repasts on sparkling tables, a foxy couple in evening dress toasting each other, a smoking pair of hot tubs—which he killed the sound on—and switched away from—coming immediately upon (and this was perfect, so he left it playing) the lion, the scarecrow, and the tin woodsman galloping away into the distance, up the Yellow Brick Road, escorting their pretty, Earthling, ruby-slippered, messianic girl in Oz—the little, bristly dog mopping up the rear—all in a candy-colored landscape of tissue paper flowers and papier-mâché tree trunks and the famous yellow paving bricks, painted flat on the plywood surface of a ramp that had been nailed together by union stagehands in a studio soundstage, which, when it existed, stood probably not far from here. In Burbank or in Hollywood. The four pilgrims skipped away together with arms interlocked, the lion's mechanized tail wiping back and forth. And when the camera lifted, it revealed the horizon where the road stretched, the city of Oz appearing there, its towers and turrets, promising to answer every desire.

He told Blythe with a wave of the remote wand, "Look, the perfect metaphor."

She couldn't pay attention because she was getting the room service people on the phone.

Metaphor for L.A. and the whole entertainment culture. Metaphor for the Fantasy Vacations biz. And for the kids' journey up the hill to touch the Hollywood Sign. Metaphor for all Bodie Lostig's delusions, too, including his vision of a future rustic Shaker Heights impoverished and utopian, but most aptly a metaphor for the boy's personal grandiosity. He, in his wheelchair, was the fuming fulminating fake wizard, handing out pronouncements. Blythe meanwhile was on the phone reaching accord with the wine people: "All right. Profound, yes, but limited. Not a wine that goes all over the place. Good. Thanks." She put the phone away, and she turned to see the TV screen he had asked her to look at. She folded her arms.

Then, having considered for an instant the metaphor on TV he'd pointed out, she turned to the wheeled cart, like a patient there, and she lifted the linen sheet, revealing carafes of water, apples and pears, cheese, a rude-woven basket filled with breads of different toughnesses and tendernesses. On ice under a glass dome was the small palette of fishy salves. The whole thing made her happy and solved all the world's problems. Lifting her arms in that same chute of fanfare in which she'd surrounded the whole operatic debacle of her dying Rod, she cried, "I am so delighted we got into all this trouble, Mark." And she took up a plate and started putting together their snacks.

Mark, in an effort to enjoy what little remained of his rancor, went straight back, "So he's some kind of anti-abortion fundamentalist."

This remark needed no prelude. The topic of Bodie was always near at hand. And the Perdue family's recent abortion was famous. Via well-intentioned gossip everybody on the tour pretty much knew why everybody else was there, and how everybody was doing.

Blythe, loading plates, didn't even glance up. "Him?" she said, puzzled. "No, no. He's Mister Liberal Everything. He and his family, they're totally Green Party, pro-choice, anti-nuclear, pro-whale . . . I think that's something you got wrong, there."

Well, if so, then he'd misunderstood. The boy would have to be entirely rethought, and reimagined.

But Mark didn't care anymore. He didn't need to understand Bodie Lostig anymore. Bodie Lostig had been effectively put away.

Mark had stopped even looking directly at Bodie Lostig's physical person, literally never again glanced, after a certain point in the evening, around the triumphal moment when $849 of his own cash, fresh from Blythe's ATM, was paid to the city and county of Los Angeles. The weekend was over, more or less, and his daughter was smart and she would soon see through him, and she would drop him. And anyway, here came a neatly composed plate of victuals.

Also, here came Blythe. She didn't sit in the armchair. She took both plates and clambered up on the bed, kneeling before him, too close, licking something savory off her finger and thumb, saying, "So. Tell me. Now at last. Why is there no such thing as 'location,'"—she shrugged one bare shoulder around at their present location, with mischief in her eye, as if there were some delicious double meaning here in the *non*existence of this particular location—"and no such thing as duration?"

She was unmistakably inside the barrier they'd agreed on. She should be sitting across the room. He said, while picking among the bits on his plate, "Oh, there is time. There is space. When I said that, I was talking about absolute measurements."

All weekend he had conveyed that, in the presence of his own ideas, he was both embarrassed and bored. Now his tone, all the more, warned her away.

In repentance—and yet somehow defiance, too—she kept her attention on her food, smiling. "We mere mortals think in relative terms, not absolutes."

There came a knock at the door and the muffled announcement "Room Service." Blythe backed away fast and got to her feet. "That was mighty quick." First she dug out of her purse a crumpled bill, and when she'd opened the door she told the short, uniformed, handsome,

Aztec-looking man how alarmingly prompt he was. The ensuing unavoidable ceremony—presenting the label, unpacking stemware and decanter, pulling the cork with a strangling grip on the bottle, pouring a sample—took place in a total silence, a sore silence, incriminating to them both. This was a different Blythe now, in her leotard-like shirt. He remembered now, the first thing she did, entering the room, was find the thermostat and turn it way up, so a hot exhaust started coming from the wall unit. The place was already growing overwarm. Mark frankly knew nothing of this woman—people can be surprising—indeed with most people, pretty much anything is possible—and if he let his imagination range back over the past days, he might find himself unmaking all his conclusions and ideas about her. He had no basis for all his assumptions. He'd gotten young Bodie Lostig all wrong, too. All bets are always off, realistically. Now, here, between two people who had but near-zero insight into *themselves*, let alone into each other, certain deeds might ensue in a hotel room, which would have consequences. The main thing he'd wanted was that there be no consequences. That shirt was somewhat halter-designed, descending from the ring of fabric at her neck and baring shoulders that were freckled as well as balletic looking. After her sample of wine was poured, she tasted it, and then she took over the bottle herself, telling the man thanks, getting him out of the room. All the while on the television screen, the quartet of supplicants, each carrying his own unique defect, or complaint, had reached the great, tall gates of Oz. The Earth-girl—the one member of the expedition who was made of flesh (rather than silvery cardboard, or straw, or costume-department notions), poor human flesh, sexual flesh, tacky-to-the-touch, indeed Kansas flesh, from right back there in the barnyard—had knocked upon the great gates. And they'd all been admitted.

Blythe had pursued the Aztec man to the door and crushed her bill into his palm, and when the door was firmly closed, she went over to the wine and turned her back, pharmacist-wise, at the table for pouring, then turned again, gloating, piloting two tall ruby wineglasses to the bed. On television—though they couldn't be heard with the sound off—the stumpy little green people were waltzing the girl through a cosmetic process that looked like a "Complete Stylist's Makeover." The colors of Oz, increasingly in every rebroadcast over the years, are radioactive, disagreeable. Kansas was better. In Kansas around the muddy barnyard everyone looked sick and pale and discouraged, like an old Swedish art film. In the atmosphere incipient tornadoes laid a dark eschatological sentence on all things. It was the Depression or something, and people were trying to seem cheerful.

Blythe, while keeping the big wineglasses from spilling, was on her knees wading up the mattress to him, reclaiming ground. She commented on Oz, waving her own heavy goblet toward the screen, "Metaphor for theoretical physics?"

Mark found that startling. And pleasing. She was playing the role of "student" so pertly. With her usual perfect clairvoyance she'd leaped forward inside his personal peculiar little philosophical world.

"How do you mean?" he said.

She sipped. "The journey to Oz: people going onward asking the *wrong* question. Dorothy and the Scarecrow and the Tin Man, all of them. They've come asking the *wrong* questions."

"Which is . . . physics . . . ?"

"As you say on the old YouTube *Nova*s." She sipped again while keeping her eyes on him. "People asking the wrong questions."

Her nearness. Her knee. It was making him panic while, inwardly, also thawing a certain syrup, syrup of disloyalty to his own life, the feeling that some stranger had replaced her, a stranger capable of flouting their agreement of prudence, and he came out and uttered a bizarre, half-baked thing, to at least stop the advance. "Funny: you want to stay loyal to 'Rod,' and I find I want to stay loyal to the little Noddy-thing idea out there. Wouldn't that be weird."

This was his cartoonish mysticism, immediately regrettable when exposed to light, something not intended in any literal way, and it would be embarrassing now if he had to try to explain, how the imaginary omniscient floating fetus had been the only constant observer of the weekend's folly. Blythe, with an absurdity thrust in her face, was making a confused effort actually to comprehend it, her gaze slowly coming apart. The remark was more of a slap than he'd meant.

So—since it also did make some kind of arcane sense—it seemed necessary to try to develop a few logical connections, and lifting a hand, gripping the strands of an invisible web, he began, "Like, how all knowledge is all connected up."

Now this was occult.

And could only get worse. "I mean, naturally, I'll always know a lot *more* things than a fetus ever did. But they'll be the same *kinds* of things. In a very general way." Yes, he was now talking Bodie Lostig's kind of philosophy, but he was entitled, unlike Bodie Lostig.

She continued to look as if she might be willing to admit there was some glimmer of a meaning there. But of course couldn't see how.

He had succeeded in one thing. He had succeeded in stopping her. In actually humiliating her, mentioning their loyalties. She'd really sat back on her heels. He'd wrecked everything.

"Of course it's huge, it's immense, the sheer *amount* of things I know because I happen to be 'alive.' I know who the president is. What color the sky is. How to walk. You know: left foot, right foot. What a hand *is*. The alphabet and the days of the week and so on." And so on, and so on. Newtonian physics and the new physics, and the even newer. What the mother Audrey's face looks like. What the weather is like on a given day.

Poor Blythe, blocked and repulsed but still kneeling before him, stared at the two plates beside her on the bed. She folded her forearms, her wineglass in the crook of an elbow, and she said, "Mark?" She was exasperated. "May I just say? It's been three months. Hasn't it? How come your whole family seems joined in this agreement to keep moaning and groaning over the Nod decision?"

"I'm so tired of that . . . name."

"You all made a logical decision." She lifted herself off her denim haunches and, avoiding looking at him, steadying herself with a hand, she was beginning the process of crawling backward on her knees, because she'd been spurned, and she climbed off the bed and went to the dresser, to add more to her glass.

Though she hadn't depleted it much. It was still mostly full.

As she poured she said, "An embryo has no consciousness. You're a scientist, Mark. You're the one who was telling *me* about survivor's guilt."

Clearly tonight he had the job—and would continue to have it— the job of belittling the offer of love. Which would be a cruel, hard insult, because he loved her. The important thing was to keep pretending it wasn't happening.

"No, not guilt," he blathered onward, "You don't understand. No guilt. Just more like *self*-pity. Like we went online and looked at all the equipment we'd need. There's this whole world online. *He* wouldn't have been eligible for any of this, but you can get helmets so they can't hurt themselves, and spoons with special handles and special exercise-gym equipment, chairs with things so they can't fall out. Video programs for home schooling—or just, I guess, pacifying them—and timing systems that put in morphine. Special little tricy-cles. There's a whole little *world*—of people devoted to these dead-end lives." His voice had been going up higher, so he stopped, then started again lower, "Of course. I'm a scientist. I believe, and I know for a fact, that it was one step up from a cyst or a wart. It possibly had a kind of 'awareness,' unlike a wart. But no *self*-awareness."

So there, he'd made that distinction aloud. It was always only an inner idea, never tested in the air. And it survived the test. Cyst or wart.

Of course, he'd always not cared, nor did anybody. That was the true and happy fact. Nobody did. People pretended to but really didn't. Not caring was the indispensable condition that originally con-densed everything out, like mass and energy in the big-bang moment. His *not* caring—and most of all his blamelessness, one's everlasting indemnity—those were the more interesting, startling aspects of the experience. Try as one might, one can't feel anything but gladness, relief, over an unremarkable little avoidance of life. And moreover, one ought not to. That was the extra thing: admitting you *don't care* you don't care. That was the strange, the additional step, decreeing a world where people don't care that people don't care. It's fine to be fine.

He summed up, "When you start implying—" he began. And then started a different way, "None of this has anything to do with guilt, or like, whether the little '*ghost*' of a baby '*forgives*' us."

Blythe, leaning there with her wineglass where she was driven away, must be getting tired of this topic this weekend. Especially now, with its obvious merely diversionary purpose.

But she did approve of that last affirmation, about how irrelevant is the forgiveness thing. She smiled mistily, "The cut worm forgives the plow?"

That seemed unlike her. He really almost recoiled. It seemed so unkind. She explained. "Poem. William Blake. The 'sad-but-true' department."

He had to wonder for a minute whether being turned away had made her bitter and now she meant to hurt him—because of the way he'd sent her from the bed. That was unkind of *him*, sending her away. That was a bad moment there. He would replay it often in memory in the weeks and months to come, and maybe even the years to come: the way she'd climbed off the bed, after having knelt before him. She, too, might always hate the memory of that moment.

But in speaking of worms and plow blades, her voice had been gentle. Her eyes had been humorous, warm, lit up. "We *are in* the sad-but-true department," she chided.

Sometimes, with Blythe, it was as if they both knew the same old tune and together they could enter up unrehearsed into it. They were conversing in a heavenly salon where nothing anymore mattered. And she was—she *was*—cold inside like him. Maybe there never had been any genuine risk of physical affection in this room—no matter how high she turn the thermostat to heat the air.

In a surge of love for her in his despair he told her, "Oh, Blythe, you know, people are pretty much interchangeable."

That perplexed her. He'd said it wrong, it sounded like he was describing an insignificance to things, a sordid insignificance. He'd meant it to be a kind of apology, just for being married to somebody else. It was as close as he would come to a confession of love.

"I don't know," she said, her eyes softened by something that made her smile a little. "You've got Audrey, and she's not interchangeable."

She intended no acrimony there. She was just ruminating, joining *him* in ruminations, upon the metaphysical mystery of separate identities. She only meant that Audrey Naale of Terra Linda—driver of a black Lexus, wearer of a red tool belt, former lawyer—didn't have these particular freckled shoulders, or the Subaru with the sticky drink holder, or hair of a certain cedar-shaving consistency, or the Risdie education, the L.A. loft with Persian carpets and a cappuccino machine. She was a different fate. It was a comment on what a comedy this is, this business of having identities, being posted at a distance from each other, each taking up the general project of being or seeming happy.

In fact he actually rather appreciated the cut-worm remark, and he went on (because he always did like to think this was fundamentally what they were talking about all weekend), "It's a good thing there *is* death, no?" The plow that comes to sever all. Death the necessary plot device in the background, to make the story go. Or death as a kind of storage place: a theater's offstage prop closet in the dark. The fetus's stunted cerebral cortex, according to the doctors, had never had any possibility of higher abstraction or language abilities. He'd often wondered, even long before this, if all you'd ever had was incomprehension and discomfort, from your earliest consciousness, you could think it was normal. You might think it's just how things are. And go on like that.

Blythe, over her wineglass rim's hoop, gave a sigh—which included a tired, formal chuckle, admitting that "death" is, yes, a sort of resource, deep and cold and dependable, irrigating all things, irrigating all the visible world. There's no afterlife, but Mark continued to enjoy the poetic and fanciful notion that when he dies he'll be "joining" the idea of Noddy, in some way. They'll simply be together in the place where $2 + 2 = 4$, that's all. The place of spare parts, the prop closet. The place where shining geometry is. And integral calculus and number theory.

Blythe was growing tired and dejected all the while—he could observe it while it was happening—because plainly the real point of all this was sinking in, that the purpose of all this talk was to replace the love she'd thought of starting. The shirt she'd chosen involved no brassiere at all, and, in the ingenious, supernatural weave of the Ace-bandage-colored stretch fabric from the magical tables of the womenswear side of the department store, her separate breasts were blinded and somehow pilloried, in a way that wounds a man, simultaneously maims and fantastically empowers him. But over this spectacle now her arms were folded. And her attention drifted to her large Celebrity tote bag.

Which she wandered over to, with a resolve. It bore the Celebrity Vacations business logo: a blazing California sun wearing sunglasses. She said, "Here you go," and she pulled out the glossy white folder, embossed with the same sun logo, whose pockets contained all the Xeroxes of the contracts, the weekend's itinerary, brochures describing the other Fantasy Vacations programs, the disclaimers he'd signed in carbon copy, contact information, order forms to fill out requesting extra CDs and DVDs and souvenir T-shirts and caps and Celebrity warm-up suits, and places for the kids to enter their email addresses and create their own online passwords to join up with the "Fame Club" website and get discounts on online games and fabulous merchandise.

She tossed it on the hotel dresser. "Your stuff," she said.

Passing it to him was a last little piece of business before getting on their flight tomorrow.

She put her wineglass on the food cart, and she took up a pear. Picking at a defect on its skin, she said, going back to the kind of talk she thought *he* preferred, "So what name would you've rathered? For the little person in memory in history."

Mark didn't answer, for suddenly he had sunk and decayed to a level where he couldn't be scraped together again. The more he taught the standard equations to undergraduates—in those classrooms where chalk dust mist in the air and chalk dust grime-paste on his palms and in his pores bred the bacteria that gave him his winter coughs and colds—the more he redescribed the old relativistic space-time geometry, the more times he went through the derivation of Planck's constant—the more fictitious became the integrals and sums, the standard Hamiltonians and de Broglies, the more irrelevant, and the more he sensed himself inside a thrumming organism where only a trustingness called ignorance got anybody by.

It was everybody's trusting ignorance, but also it was his case particularly. The antibiotics had worked, but there were still episodes, and always would be, when he couldn't remember the commonest word; or in a journal article, an equation on the page would stand eternally mocking his understanding; or when the first half of a sentence, which he had no idea how to finish, extended like a pier, out into a misty lake. Only tenure kept him standing.

Blythe shrugged. "I had an abortion. Long ago. College. But it wasn't late-term."

Mark said, "Mm." It was supposed to be a noise of empathy. He picked up his plate and set it on his lap and broke a piece of bread. His life had pretty much passed him by. He ought to be hungry, and *was* hungry, but also finishing his meal was like a kind of progress, or just impatience.

On television the four seekers in Oz were still aiming to get to the halls of enlightenment. Dorothy was being drawn on a horse cart by a green horse through the streets of an Emerald City like an old Bavarian village. Probably Judy Garland had abortions, too, sleeping her way through Hollywood at some point in her career. Possibly—or even certainly?—such things happened back then.

"Everybody's had an abortion," he said in commiseration. Also if it wasn't late-term it would have been a whole different thing. Maybe it would have been better if they *had* viewed the remains. In the days before the operation, a nurse at a desk with a computer and a gliding mouse (a mouse that clicked and circled, while she filled out an onscreen form), had asked whether they would like to view the remains. Mark and Audrey were slightly horrified, but according to the nurse some people with late-terms insist on viewing the remains. The Perdues naturally did not need to, and they said so. And so a click went into the mouse under the nurse's hand, which created the computer record, and the mouse went circling and clicking, and the question never came up again. It was a good thing in fact, because he didn't want to see the remains and the sight could have done no good for anybody. He would have just pictured a kind of slippery chute somewhere. (If it were necessary to picture anything!)

Blythe stopped watching TV—the little green horse, as it pulled the cart, was tossing its shampooed head—and she again topped off her glass, and she turned and came back to the bed, bringing her wineglass with her, and on her knees slid up toward the same place as before, while Mark kept watching the screen.

She set her wineglass aside and focused on him. He kept his eyes on the TV. But she'd planted herself to make a sizeable notch in his lane of vision, kneeling, hands on hips, shoulders pressed back. He was aware, sidewise, of the lichen-green color in her gaze in hotel lamp-light, and he knew that she must be seeing what everybody saw: a man who, objectively, wasn't going to be pulling his weight anymore, and in the midst of this desert he'd entered, she saw herself as medicine. She *lived* in this particular desert here. It was her desert. Where he was a newcomer, she was a creature adapted to it, its austerities, its compromises, privations. And now here she was on the bed: she had made herself now a lower-class sort of woman for him, a second-best, low-self-esteem, out-of-town woman. It was unmistakable that the unbrassiered breasts were a gift, swaddled as they were in the stretch fabric that suspended each separately in sight, heavily, to deliver the old never-fail mental concussion, putting the crucial dab of Novocain upon a man's brain—for Mark was a creature helplessly evolved to obey any whatsoever tides or gravitational yearnings; and already *always, whenever* he was around her, he was aware of the inevitable prickle of the deep roots' clutch, a grip on his body furnished by evolution for purposes of reproduction but also, accidentally-on-purpose, an addictive pleasure, like that of a lab rat who will keep pressing the bar to get the sweet pellet, and she of course must know he was constrained to that. The empty void she evoked in the world around herself was the drug, as well as the license, it was the beginning of mercy, it was the condition of his deliverance.

He turned fatally to look in her eyes.

And she said, "All right, I've got to go. So gimme an innocent little kiss, dear Mark. It's two-something by now."

"Two-something. Why, the night's only beginning."

She rolled her eyes. All this was the perfect melting road. Now they could simply *be* unwise, and forgetful, and allow face to drift closer to face, and he would start to *accept* that form of airless underwater delirium and would be unzipping those jeans and releasing the sight of her hip rising. It could happen any time he liked. The two breasts actually seemed to swell under his sight (if that were physiologically possible), and he murmured as he kept an eye on them, "And anyway the movie's not over." His plate was there, and he broke off a piece of bread, thinking it might be debonair—to chew on a little bit of bread, prolonging the flirtation cruelly.

She said, "I have a feeling Lotta and Bodie *will* decide they want to do the video tomorrow. So in the morning I'll be here at nine to pick you up. Okay? As planned? You're not going to have much time to get some sleep in."

So he made his move. As bold as any handsome cinema actor, he fastened the starfish of his hand to her left breast and, suavely, gave it a couple of fond little pulses. But he certainly must have misunderstood the situation. Because she yipped his name and batted his hand away and sat up straighter, smiling crazily. Then she seized the same hand she had just knocked away. She held it down on her thigh in both her hands. "You are such a goof," she sang. "It's flattering, Mark. It is. It really is." She was petting his hand, petting it hard, because *it* had misbehaved. The attack had gone off wrong. He'd seen right away by the light in her eye—by her thrilled horror—the little squeezes he'd given the breast were more like a double-honk on a rubber bulb. That's what her unnecessary, hysterical, spastic response made of the situation.

Still, it would be possible to recover somehow. He'd hung his head sharp to one side. As if a neck tendon had been clipped. And he looked down and, with a free hand, painted his torn bread crust in the salmon mousse, then taking a bite, he smiled up at her, trying to show shameless, unrepentant cunning.

She seemed to take the smile as sorriness. She smiled back at him, shaking her head, "You really are a goof," and she lifted his captive hand, squeezing it into a fist between her own, pressing it to a safe spot between her breasts.

If it were possible, by a deep-enough sigh, to rewind time just twenty seconds, Mark drew exactly such a sigh now. It was a great sigh that might *succeed* in sucking back events while they still lingered in the air between them. But he inhaled a flake of breadcrust and he had to cough, right in her face, pushing back against the headboard to launch it out. It was a big high-velocity cough, and he *was* able to keep the entire mouthful from exploding all over her, but then he had to gasp, because a second cough was coming, and the intake of breath sucked something deep in his air passage. Bread. It was so well plugged in his throat, he couldn't make a sound. He looked at her. Eyes alone could communicate. A vacuum-seal had shut him out from life. It had put him behind a pane. Right before his face was the air he needed: his eyes swam forward in the very oxygen. But seeing it alone wasn't enough. This would be serious. The wad of bread was really well stuck.

Blythe saw what was wrong right away, and she stood up from the bed. He could, in fact, make little sounds in his larynx, but they were a dead man's sounds. And the effort pinched his esophagus tighter. He didn't like this at all. This was the kind of thing you *hear* about. He climbed forward and crouched on all fours like a vomiting dog. But that posture did nothing to pop out the plug. The wad of bread was really not moving. There was nothing going in and nothing coming out, neither ebb nor flow of air. Meanwhile his brain seemed to be

211

ballooning inside his skull. Blythe came over and started banging on his spine.

That did nothing. It was just an annoyance. It just hurt. He crawled away from the rain of blows, trying to bank what little oxygen he had in his lungs. For some reason Blythe went into the bathroom. Obviously she was in an irrational state of not knowing how to act. Because she came right back out. He got to his feet on the floor. He had an idea he should run out into the corridor, and maybe get to the lobby. But that would accomplish nothing. Blythe was saying, "What should I do? What do you want me do to?" She picked up the phone, but he waved at her to put it down, because he was a married man in a hotel room with a young woman who was so well-dressed, at two-something in the morning, with wine. That's where he was, whether dead *or* alive.

They both, surely, knew about the Heimlich maneuver. He made embracing motions, nodding his head. She understood and she approached—daintily, as if he were soaking wet and she didn't want to dampen her own clothes—and she started hugging him face-to-face. She didn't know how to do it. You're supposed to hug people from behind. But he had trouble prying her away. He himself was getting weak. He was trying to conserve energy. She understood and moved away.

He turned around and backed into her. She locked her forearms over his ribcage, over the heart area, and began constricting as hard as she could. This wasn't going to work. The pressure had the effect of locking down, all the more, the plug in his throat. That plug was the floor of his consciousness now. That plug represented the silent seafloor where he was planted and still waving. She kept on hugging, tighter, because it might work eventually.

On the desk by the phone, two paper sleeves held the return flight tickets. He could see them right there, while she squeezed and hugged, see them with eyes that were still functioning. It was an image carried by optic nerves to a brain that wasn't yet oxygen-deprived. He almost felt that if he ceased to exist, Lotta and Audrey would cease to exist, too! As if *they* were a pair of people he'd dreamed up in the process of dreaming himself up.

Of course the truth was, they were real, actual people. Who would have to go on without him. Into the future. A remark came back to him: it was something he'd told Lotta tonight, when she was whining over how small was the chance of her having come to exist at all, *There's always going to be a you.* It was only a throwaway remark, like a joke, but it had a joke's grain-of-truth quality, too, accidentally, the way a bell, in chiming, does summon eternity. That *"there's 'always' going to be a 'you'"* would be as true for Lotta as it had been for him.

This entire end-of-the-world business of "personal extinction" had always been only an abstraction, something that happened to other people, people who *were* only dreamed up as accessories in his own existence. When death isn't a remote abstraction anymore, you see how the whole design would be unfair, if that's how it works, and the arrangement itself ought to be frankly addressed, not only on the general principle of justice, but also in view of a more efficient design in nature. The purity of being right about this ought to be invincible. On the television screen (because his vision was starting to shrink and he was going back to being merely an inconsequential visitor again in this life) was the palace of the Wizard, its lustrous floors. The quartet of timid pilgrims, each clutching tightly his own personal defect, were entering upon the long corridor, to make their entreaties of the fraudulent Oz—only to learn in the end, of course, they'd got it wrong, because they *were*, yes, asking the wrong questions. What they were seeking had never existed, and wasn't even desirable. What they needed was behind them somewhere, something very small, something they'd left back in the grass somewhere long ago. Old story. This movie was another of the million things a fetus would never know about. Would never suspect the existence of. Most things were like that: their existence unsuspected. All our lives, mere tangency suffices for touch. One ought not to be astonished, or pretend it's a big surprise. The only great experiences were Audrey and Lotta. Whom however he'd, likewise, hardly known. They had slipped through his "hands." As does it all. And he had been remiss, too, in the matter of the goldfish. The thing had been on his mind. Because if that fish were, in fact, swimming right now in a glass of water beside a bathroom mirror, it *wouldn't* be able to take comfort in thinking its reflection was a companion, swimming alongside. Every time it took a turn, its little friend would fail to follow. What schooling fish need is to stay parallel. Instead, with a mirror's reverse symmetries, its only friend would keep peeling away. Peeling away forever. Which could drive a goldfish mad, in eternity.

Then Mark was aware that he could breathe. His forehead was on the carpet and he could breathe. He was lying on the carpet. He was lucky. He worked steadily at breathing. And just let Blythe wait. Then he lifted his head. The wad of bread was out there in the room somewhere. He had fainted. Blythe had, in the meantime, come around to sit before him cross-legged on the floor, looking out of breath herself. She had figured out the Heimlich maneuver.

★ SHE STAYED FOR only a little while. She made tea, of some pointless tasteless herbal type; the hotel provided an electric kettle on the bathroom counter with a basket of tea bags. During much of the time waiting for the kettle to heat, she stayed out of sight in the bathroom, watching it get hot.

Mark didn't want any tea, but because she was having a cup, he accepted a cup of his own and had a sip or two. It was good to have the heat spreading over his heart. She sat across the room in the armchair. "I squeezed the stomach. Instead of the chest. That's the secret."

It was a remark that ended a long silence. It was as if everything they'd said in the last three days were lies, even though they'd sincerely believed it all, and it all must have been true at the time. It all *was* true. He'd turned the TV off, so they were more alone. "Interesting day tomorrow," Blythe said. "The video things. The little awards ceremony, the good-byes, the hugs in the parking lot."

She was going to keep the conversation superficial, nurse-like—escort-like.

He went ahead and said a necessary thing that wasn't superficial. "Well, you saved my life." It came out as superficial, surprisingly so.

She smiled. "Well, this *tea* is definitely . . ." she said. And then went for the cliché, "Just what the doctor ordered."

"It's delicious."

It tasted like hot water. But that was fine.

"What airline are you going out on tomorrow?"

"I'm not sure," he said. "Southwest."

"Good. Good. That's what I thought." She sipped her tea. "That's easy. It's the first terminal you come to."

She looked around the room and set down her cup, with a clink on the glass tabletop. The jacket she'd taken off was strewn across a big square ottoman, and she leaned far over the arm of the chair to snag it. And put it on.

"Well, *that's* all something I guess I'll never tell anybody about," Mark said.

"Ha," she said, zipping up her jacket. "I suppose you'll never have an occasion."

"An occasion?" He didn't understand.

"An occasion to bring it up," she explained. "It wouldn't come up in casual conversation."

She picked up her tea, and she started plugging away again at getting it all down.

"No." Mark was watching her in a state of gratitude. But gratitude for more than just the Heimlich maneuver. "It wouldn't."

"What wouldn't?" He'd taken so long to respond.

"It wouldn't come up in casual conversation."

She stared down into her teacup, and then took another swallow. After a minute, she said with mild amusement, "No, it wouldn't."

"Tell me," Mark said, "What *albums* does Rod's guitar playing appear on? Would I know any of them? Did he play with anybody famous?"

"Oh yeah, he's on some real stars' albums. Like huge megapeople. You wouldn't have heard of any of them but they're big names."

"Like who?"

"Nobody you'd know, though. It's a different world."

"Well, they're stars, aren't they? Try me. When I get home I could buy the albums and hear Rod's guitar playing."

She lowered her teacup and started listing, "Loxy Standish . . . ? Road Rash . . . ? Tim Glennon . . . ? Tim Glennon was in the Deceivers in the '80s. Tory Amberson? She's huge."

Mark had to roll his eyes. "Sorry."

She smiled. "Well, it's all available. It's all out there. I'll bring some CDs for you tomorrow. For you to take with."

Her cup was all empty now. She lowered it to the glass of the coffee table without making a click. The thick book of hotel amenities was there, and she aligned its edge with the table edge, square upon the glossy visitor's-guide magazine, just exactly as the housekeeping staff had aligned it the Friday before, before this guest's check-in, and then each afternoon, in maids' visits, realigned it. Blythe patted her own knees, twice, lightly, and said the words *Gotta go.*

And so he would see her to the door. There was still tomorrow. On the threshold they put their arms around each other and avoided looking at each other; they were so much like children who'd gotten in trouble. But then their eyes met, and for that instant, they seemed almost to share a little soft mirth and shame, then they exchanged the see-you-tomorrow words, and she went.

Closing the door, he turned back to his empty room. This would feel good now, the recovery of his place. And turning his mind to Lotta and Audrey and Berkeley. Reinhabiting his solitude. That was fast, getting rid of her. She would be descending, too, in relief at the efficiency of the goodbye, the refusal to linger and dwell. All they might have dwelt on was how meaningless, in the end, had been their days of flirtation. He always did want to get back to his wife, and Blythe always wanted to go on alone. That little admission had been in their eyes, there at the threshold: that they were lucky how meaningless it had been. So blessedly weak is man's heart that meaninglessness is his constant rescue. Philosophers pretend meaninglessness is a bad thing. Instead, the ignorance and the shallowness are the medium that buoys us up. They exalt us every instant. There were his pajamas, the ones Audrey had given him last year. And his toothbrush was in the bathroom. One reaches out and touches things, gets ahold of things, and thus gets orientation.

Shirt buttons needed to be—one at a time—with a twist and a pinch—undone. Pants pockets needed to be emptied. The eight ibuprofen tablets—four from each pocket—were laid out in on the tabletop in a symmetrical ring around his wallet.

When he inserted himself inside the taut cool envelope of a hotel bed, he knew sleep would come fast. His tired mind would begin its old corkscrewing motion, taking root. The sensation that one has a "self" blossoms, and then dissolves. His throat, inside, was a little bruised. But air flowed in and out. Looking forward to tomorrow, he could imagine and almost literally *feel*—because you do get things just about in the form you envision them—*feel* the pressure of the airplane seat against his spine on takeoff, when, on the 5:05 PM flight in seat 8A with Lotta beside him, the inertial g-forces would pull him into the airlines' upholstery, cradling him in acceleration, and he and his daughter would be lifted forward to San Francisco. He would regret nothing when, tomorrow, he watched the great city fall away below him in its mellow air, the city that would always hold Blythe Cress, then the great white sickle would slice slow under the plane, and the glittering blue ocean would tilt. That two plus two would eternally equal four—and always, eternally, *had* equaled four, even in the emptiness before the beginning of time—would always feel like a column of light standing in his heart. Even if there were only a vacuum. He was impatient like a child to mention it to Audrey. See if she comes back with anything. Because it was interesting, and it seemed like good news, and it was beautiful, it had immanent beauty in the mathematician's sense, as if the principle alone furnished the kind of radiance to have made matter originally bead up out of nothing. The whole feeling, in general, could almost make him wish he'd gone to Karlsruhe, but he didn't yet want to confess an oddball new idea to anybody. If he knows anything, he knows he will continue for some while with no clear feeling about this number idea. It might be a problem. It might be a serious problem.